Karin Baine lives in Northern Ireland with her husband, two sons and her out-of-control notebook collection. Her mother and her grandmother's vast collection of books inspired her love of reading and her dream of becoming a Mills & Boon author. Now she can tell people she has a *proper* job! You can follow Karin on Twitter, @karinbaine1, or visit her website for the latest news—karinbaine.com.

Also by Karin Baine

French Fling to Forever
A Kiss to Change Her Life
The Doctor's Forbidden Fling
The Courage to Love Her Army Doc
Falling for the Foster Mum
Reforming the Playboy
Their Mistletoe Baby
From Fling to Wedding Ring

Discover more at millsandboon.co.uk.

MIDWIFE UNDER THE MISTLETOE

KARIN BAINE

MILLS & BOON

First Published in Great Britain 2018
by Mills & Boon, an imprint of HarperCollins*Publishers*
1 London Bridge Street, London, SE1 9GF

© 2018 Karin Baine

ISBN: 978-0-263-93382-6

MIX
Paper from
responsible sources
FSC C007454

This book is produced from independently certified FSC™ paper
to ensure responsible forest management.
For more information visit www.harpercollins.co.uk/green.

Printed and bound in Spain
by CPI, Barcelona

For Catherine, Chellie, Julia and Laurie,
who helped me get this book into shape,
and a shout out to Aunt Sadie and Nigel.

A donation has been made to an ICP charity
on behalf of my sister Jemma's 'little itch'—Maisie.

CHAPTER ONE

'ANYONE WOULD THINK I had baby brain,' Iona muttered as she retrieved her perfectly good pen from the bin, where she'd tossed it along with the wet paper towel.

'Are you sure you don't?' Della, her heavily pregnant last appointment of the day, enquired with a grin.

'I'm one hundred percent positive on that score.' You needed to have had *some* sort of relations in order for that to happen and Iona had been a born-again virgin since moving to the tranquillity of the Scottish Highlands. A serious relationship was the last thing she wanted to get entangled in when she was just beginning to get her life together at last.

Although baby brain wasn't an actual recognised medical condition Iona did believe the to-do list for mothers and mothers-to-be could easily push other thoughts from mind. Her lapses in memory today were more likely to be new-house brain. She'd received the keys to her first non-share, non-rented flat this morning and couldn't wait to finish work and go home for the first time.

'That's a shame. I was hoping for a buddy to go to mother and baby club with at the church hall.'

'Sorry to disappoint. Maybe when you're planning baby number three we can co-ordinate our schedules.'

Iona took the teasing with a pinch of salt because a child

of her own was never going to happen. She loved the innocence of a newborn and the pure joy they brought to families and had her personal experiences been different she would've loved to have been a mother herself.

Unfortunately, having a baby meant tying yourself to the father for the rest of your life, with no escape, and she wouldn't trust another man enough to make that sort of commitment again. She'd seen her parents caught in that trap, persevering with a long-dead marriage for the sake of their child, until they'd ended up resenting each other. In her effort to escape the toxic atmosphere she'd attached herself much too young to the dashing Andy, marrying him straight out of school. Only to find herself in an abusive relationship that she knew she would never have left if children had been involved too. It had taken her long enough just to get herself out of it.

No, Iona was happy to remain on the spectator side of pregnancy as a midwife. She was keen to help and support mothers until their babies had been safely delivered and monitor them for as long as they needed it, but her obligation didn't go beyond a medical capacity. At the end of the day the babies went home with their mothers and she wasn't beholden to anyone but herself and her job. She hadn't gone back to school and spent years retraining as a midwife to throw it all away for another man.

Della laughed, clutching her beachball belly. There was definitely a glow in the women who came to the clinic to see Iona and whilst she might experience a pang of regret she'd never get to go through the joys of pregnancy herself, she'd accepted it. Conventional motherhood dictated a lifestyle she wasn't prepared to give up her newfound freedom for.

She dipped the test paper into her patient's urine sample and checked it against the colour chart for analysis. 'Hmm, there's a slight trace of protein. Excess protein can be a sign of a urinary tract infection so we'll have to keep an eye on that in future appointments and if you experience any other symptoms, let me know straight away. Other than that, I'd say pregnancy is agreeing with you.'

Protein in the urine could also be an indicator of kidney damage or other disorders, including pre-eclampsia, but since Della's blood pressure was normal and this was the first sign of a problem, Iona didn't deem it necessary to worry her. If repeat tests showed similar readings she would send a sample to the lab for testing.

She tossed the used stick in the bin and gave her hands another wash. After Dr Irvine's retirement she'd been temporarily upgraded to using this room to treat her patients. Although she was glad of the extra space, she had been sorry to see him go. The senior GP partner—whom she suspected had been practising medicine when Highlanders had still roamed these hills—had made the decision to take her on here at the clinic permanently. It was a position for which she'd be grateful for ever when it had provided her with the financial independence she'd long dreamed about.

Jim, as he'd insisted she call him, had been a true gent with an old-school approach to treating his patients. He'd known everyone in Culcranna by name and had always had time for those who'd needed him. As a result, he'd been well loved and respected. Only time would tell about his replacement, Dr McColl, who'd taken over as senior partner now Jim was content to spend his retirement on the golf course.

Although Fraser McColl was closer to her age than his predecessor, there was a stern quality in his manner that put her on edge and had caused a few run-ins between them. The latest had been his decision to cancel the staff Christmas party usually held on the premises out of hours. He'd called it unprofessional, made noises about it not being covered by insurance and she'd fought him on the issue because she'd been so looking forward to experiencing the tradition she'd heard so much about. Her colleagues had made the annual shindig sound so much fun she'd imagined it would be the perfect way to mark her first Christmas in the village.

Fraser had refused to back down, probably because he'd never understand how much her new job and new home meant to her. By all accounts he came from a family of means, with land and a title to boot, so a tiny flat and a steady income were probably inconsequential to him when they were everything to Iona.

Despite her rallying cry to the rest of the staff to protest, Fraser had imposed so many restrictions on the celebrations they'd been forced into a staid dinner at the nearest restaurant instead. Iona thought his stance on the matter was more about him letting the power go to his head than any insurance issues and had told him so in a fit of pique.

Since then they'd had a few minor rows, more to do with their clash of personalities than to any professional discourse. Iona didn't appreciate anyone imposing unjustified restrictions on her after enduring a lifetime of that with her ex, and apparently Fraser didn't gel well with people who didn't fall into line. Which was tough luck for him because she was no longer prepared to tailor who she was to suit the needs of others.

There was no doubting Fraser's skills or popularity as one of the practice doctors but his tendency to take over certain situations wasn't a character trait she was keen on these days. With his dark, wavy hair and piercing green eyes he certainly cut a dashing figure in the sleepy village that even Iona wasn't immune to. Whilst he had some of the local ladies hot under their cardigans, he reminded her of the men in her past who'd tried to stunt her personal growth. There was too much apparent control freakery about him for her to drop her defences, or any item of clothing, and she hated herself for finding him remotely attractive.

Perhaps if he kept his mouth shut she could enjoy the view at least, without having her hackles raised along with her pulse.

'You wouldn't be saying that if you saw me in the wee hours of the morning, running to the loo every five minutes, or when my insides are on fire with heartburn.' Della shuffled her bottom to the edge of the chair before attempting to get to her feet, trying to balance the extra weight she was carrying around her middle.

Iona gave her a hand rather than watch her struggle like a turtle flipped onto its back, trying to right itself.

'Well, you haven't long to go now. I'll see you in a couple of weeks if you don't go into labour before then.' They'd discussed Della having to be induced if she went too far past her predicted due date but as this was her second pregnancy with no previous complications, Iona wasn't expecting she would require medical intervention.

'Thanks. I can't wait to have this little bundle in my arms.' That tender belly-rub every mother-to-be performed in here made Iona think about her own mum and the excitement she must've felt before her impending birth. A woman didn't carry and protect her baby for nine months expecting they'd both end up trapped in a life neither of them wanted.

She swallowed the rising sob in her chest. They were both free from those soul-destroying relationships now. It was just a tragedy it had come at the price of her mother's death.

'Your daughter will be here soon enough.' Iona handed Della's antenatal notes back to her with a smile. This was supposed to be a happy time for both of them. She had her own baby to get back to—her shiny new flat—and since they were three-quarters of the way through December she'd even treated herself to some new Christmas decorations. Some might say she'd gone overboard but she had enough to brighten up this dreary place too and really mark her first Christmas in the village.

'I need these bloods sent off to the lab, there's a pile of hospital referrals that need to be chased up, and this is Mrs Robertson's prescription. Her husband's going to call in before closing. I've informed him we usually require forty-eight hours for repeat prescriptions and we can't keep on doing this.'

'But she is eighty-three and we have to make allowances,' Sheila, Fraser's secretary, reminded him as she took the stack of paperwork from him with a nod and set it on her desk.

'It doesn't mean I have to be happy about it.' He had enough to do without these last-minute requests to deal with too.

Taking on the role of senior partner brought with it a lot of extra form filling and bureaucracy but it was a position he revelled in. It gave him an extra say in how the practice was run and that would make him infinitely happier in his work. Structure and boundaries gave him a sense of security, an assurance he was doing things right. It was when he strayed from the rules that things fell apart. Okay, so he was no longer that over-active little boy whose parents had sent him to boarding school so he wouldn't disturb his sick mother, but he'd learned his lesson since then. If he played by the rules there was a place for him and things would work out fine. Now he simply had to get everyone else to fall in line with him.

Not all of Jim Irvine's practices adhered with that idea of running a smooth clinic. Now, there was a man who hadn't bothered too much about form filling or adhering to schedules. That kind of reckless approach had led to inevitable chaos and caused a run-on effect that could have seen the practice run into the ground if not for Fraser picking up the slack to keep the place afloat.

At least Sheila, his second-in-command, who'd been here since the year dot, appreciated how hard he was working to make these changes a success and could be relied on to keep on top of things. Sure, some of his forward-thinking ideas were going to rub a few members of staff up the wrong way. One particular community midwife with chestnut-coloured curls, who thrived on challenging his authority, sprang to mind, having made it clear she preferred his predecessor's slap dash ethos to his.

When Iona had first started working at the clinic Fraser had been pleased they'd drafted in some new blood to bring some modern thinking into the outdated practice and lower the average age of the village population at the same time. There weren't many single, young women in the vicinity but if he'd harboured any nonsensical ideas about finding someone else to settle down with again, Iona had put paid to that with her rebellion against his attempts to bring some structure to the practice.

She refused to attend his weekly meetings regarding the cleaning rota for the staffroom on the basis she ate her meals in her car and was solely responsible for its upkeep. Then there was the argument they'd had over the clutter Iona seemed to accumulate in her room. She'd told him in no uncertain terms that it was her territory and as long as it was clean and functional it was not Fraser's concern.

It seemed Iona preferred to tackle problems as they came in rather than pre-empt them. He'd been there with Caroline, his last girlfriend, and wasn't prepared to go through it again. Caroline had let him imagine they had a future together, planning that happy family with him he'd long been denied. Only she'd decided at the last minute it wasn't what she wanted at all and had blamed him for apparently not being true to her, or himself. Whatever that meant.

So he'd ploughed all of his energy back into work instead of the domestic bliss he'd been promised. He wasn't going to let another flighty woman steal his dreams from him when a new efficient way of working would better serve patients and staff alike.

Whether Iona Munro liked it or not, his new system was getting results. His last patient had been and gone and he was finishing for the day bang on time. Simply by sticking to the ten-minute time slots for each appointment, everything was running like clockwork. He'd say that was a resounding success and a score for all of the Type A personalities out there.

'I'll get on to these straight away, Dr McColl,' Sheila called after him since he'd already left the main office to check all patients had left the premises. At this time of the evening, as the working day was winding down, the hubbub outside the treatment rooms had usually died down, but there were still a few voices ringing out from the reception area. Any out-of-hours emergencies now should have been referred to the hospital or the doctor on call for the area.

The notion that his perfectly executed schedule had been thrown into disarray ploughed grooves across Fraser's forehead even before he was met with the debacle in the waiting area.

'Lift your side up a little higher. Left a bit. How does that look now? Is it straight?' Iona was balanced on a chair, trying to pin a gaudy gold-foil garland to the ceiling, with Victoria, the receptionist, as her partner in crime.

'What the—?' Fraser stopped dead in his tracks at the sight of Iona, barefoot and on tiptoe, breaking every health and safety rule in the workplace. He was in danger of hyperventilating as he did a quick risk assessment of the scene.

'Oh, hi, Fraser. I thought we could brighten the place up and make it look less sterile in here.' Unlike the rest of the staff, who quickly made themselves scarce, Iona carried on decorating as though she was perfectly entitled to do as she pleased. It was one thing managing her own caseload but she didn't have any authority outside that.

'It's supposed to be sterile!' Fraser didn't want to lose his temper when that would be a sign he wasn't in control. Although the garish garlands draped across every available space, transforming the beige room into an eyesore of gold and red, hinted he hadn't asserted his authority here as much as he'd believed.

'Lighten up, Fraser. It's Christmas. If you're worried about the cost, it's coming from my own pocket, not yours.

'Fraser.' This was exactly why she rubbed him up the wrong way. Iona gave no thought for the rules or decorum in the workplace, or anywhere else for that matter. The patients loved her easygoing persona but for Fraser that free spirit vibe was unsettling, as was anything that didn't fit into his idea of conformity. It upset that safe environment he was trying to set up here, and quite frankly he didn't know how to handle it.

Fraser had mistakenly believed Caroline had been the one person who'd understood him when they'd made their plans to get married and settle down into quiet family life, but when his father had died and he'd inherited the family estate he'd discovered the truth. Once Fraser had the means to make those dreams a reality Caroline had confessed they'd been nothing more than an idea she'd been paying lip service to, not a legitimate option. That level of deception had ultimately ended their relationship and Fraser's hope for the future.

This was different, though. Iona wasn't a love interest, so her casual attitude to life shouldn't bother him on a personal level, but she was a staff member and they had rules in place here for a reason.

'I appreciate the gesture,' Fraser said diplomatically, doing his best to remain calm. Iona didn't know him personally so wouldn't understand the issues he had with the whole palaver at this time of the year.

They'd never gone in for the whole over-the-top lead up to Christmas at boarding school and the death of his mother on Christmas Eve had cemented Fraser's dislike of the season. It was a reminder of the childhood he'd lost and the family that had never recovered from the devastation of cancer. Now he dreaded that last week in December more than ever since it was also the anniversary of his break-up with Caroline.

He'd made the mistake of trying to embrace Christmas last year in an effort to make it special for her with an over-the-top marriage proposal, including a horse-drawn sleigh and carol singers serenading them along the ride. Only she'd turned him down on the basis that he was 'being fake'. Fraser couldn't win and was now even less likely to get caught up in the fuss, reverting back to his true Grinchy self, unwilling to be one of those people who lost their minds for the sake of one anti-climactic day.

On the rare occasions his parents had retrieved Fraser for the holidays it had been a non-event anyway. They'd gone through the motions without ever getting bogged down in the sentiment. Whilst he'd yearned for this infantile nonsense as a child far from home, he'd learned to live without it.

Iona carried on making her mark on the recently painted ceiling, humming Christmas carols and reminding Fraser what a very long month December could be when you weren't in the festive spirit.

'As I said, I appreciate the gesture but we can't have all

of this cluttering up the surgery.' He would've told her that if she'd sought his permission in the first place.

'I think the patients will love it. It gives them something to focus on other than their aches and pains.'

Sure. They'd all end up with tinsel blindness on top of everything else.

'I'm sorry, it'll all have to go. It's a health and safety hazard.' Fraser began to detach the string of fairy lights from the reception desk.

'Okay, I'll give you the lights. They haven't been assessed by a registered electrician but they are bonny. Perhaps I could bung more tinsel there instead. I have some neon pink somewhere...' Iona clearly wasn't going to give this up without a fight and, as had become the custom, Fraser would have to get tough to have his opinion heard.

He ripped down the cardboard Father Christmas she'd stuck to the counter and hoped it wouldn't leave any sticky marks behind. 'It's all going to have to come down.'

Iona stopped this time. 'You're kidding me, right?'

'I don't kid.' He reached his hand up and tugged the large blue and silver foil star dangling from the ceiling until the tack holding it in place dislodged and pinged to the floor. This was exactly what he was talking about. One drawing pin in the wrong person's foot and they could be facing a lawsuit. Luckily for them both he spotted the gold pin glinting on the dark carpet and retrieved it before it damaged more than his peace of mind.

'What harm can a few decorations do?' Iona faced him, her displeasure flaring in her big brown eyes and her full lips pursed into a tight line. It didn't thrill him to note he was the one with the power to steal away the twinkling smile she wore for everyone else.

'They're a breeding ground for germs with so many sick people coming and going. Then there's the dust. Think of how many asthma patients we have. Our appointment list is full enough without putting it under more stress.' Deep down Fraser knew he was grasping for excuses but coming into the clinic every morning and being reminded of the worst days of his life was too much for him to bear.

'Okay. Okay. I get it. I was only trying to do something nice. Talk about dampening the mood,' she muttered as though he wasn't there, and began dismantling her ceiling display.

'I know, but perhaps next time you could check with me first instead of going rogue?' Fraser understood her intentions had been good and would've preferred not to fuel this animosity between them, but Iona's spur-of-the-moment actions were infuriating when they impeached on his carefully laid plans and tugged on emotions that needed to remain dormant for the remainder of this dreaded month.

'Yes, sir.' With her anger clearly still bubbling away, Iona yanked down the bunting she'd only finished hanging.

Fraser watched in horror as she tottered on the chair, clearly off balance, her arms freewheeling in the air as she fell.

With lightning-fast reflexes he rushed over and caught her in his arms before she hit the floor. Iona's yelp softened to a gasp as he hooked a hand under her knees and one under her arms. Instinctively she latched her arms around his neck but that contact and the strong grip she had on him almost startled him into dropping her again.

The adrenaline rush was making them both breathe heavily and in that moment, holding her in his arms, their faces almost touching, it was easy to forget what they'd been fighting over, or even where they were.

She weighed very little, reminding him how delicate she appeared to be beyond the bravado. Despite her petite frame, she projected herself as a larger-than-life character but, with their clashing personalities stripped away for the time being, he was reacting solely as a man with an attractive woman pressed against him and was too stunned to do anything other than enjoy the sensation.

Iona blinked first. 'You can put me down now. I think I'm safe.'

'Sure.' Fraser abruptly set her back on her feet and tried to compose himself. 'Like I said, a health and safety nightmare.'

He ignored her tutting as she tore down the rest of the decorations, thankful that this moment of madness had passed, letting normal, tense service resume between them. It was easier to view her as a threat to his plans for a new, improved workplace than through any inappropriate romantic haze.

CHAPTER TWO

As she did every morning, Iona arrived at the clinic with plenty of time to spare before she was officially on the clock. Due to the unpredictable nature of midwifery, scheduled meal breaks were impossible and she often had to eat on the road, if she managed to eat at all. So having a quick cup of tea and a bowl of porridge in the morning as she checked her schedule for the day ensured Iona had at least one proper meal in peace.

Today she was especially keen to get on the road as she'd booked the afternoon off. It was moving day and she was bursting with the excitement of transferring her belongings from her rental to her very own home. It wouldn't take more than a few runs in the car with the meagre possessions she had, and some of her male colleagues had volunteered to give her a hand with the heavy lifting. The sooner Iona got around her patients, the sooner she'd get settled into her own place.

Except as she lifted her first spoonful of thick, oaty goodness to her mouth, a note in the blood results of one of her patients immediately threw her plans into chaos. Iona shovelled in her breakfast as quickly as she could while digesting the news that had come in.

At around five days old, babies were offered newborn blood spot screening, or a heel-prick test, where a small amount of blood is taken to screen for certain genetic disorders. In this case, the baby had tested positive for one of the listed conditions—phenylketonuria, or PKU for short. Although Iona had done some research into the illness during the course of her training, it was a rare metabolic condition she'd never personally come across before, with approximately only one baby in ten thousand in the UK a sufferer.

The genetic mutation for phenylketonuria was passed on by both parents who might not even have been aware they were carriers. PKU patients, unable to break down the amino acid phenylalanine, a building block of protein, could have a build-up of protein leading to brain damage without adherence to a strict low-protein diet. It was imperative the child be referred to the metabolic unit at the hospital as soon as possible to begin treatment and prevent any long-term damage.

Although modern advances thankfully kept the condition under control with the restricted diet and amino acid supplement to ensure normal development, Iona was aware the news would have a great impact on the family. Every new mum wanted to believe her baby was perfect and to be told otherwise could be difficult to accept and overwhelming.

She took a gulp of tea before pouring the rest down the sink and gave the dishes a quick rinse. There wasn't liable to be a spare minute today but she had one more thing to do before she could hit the road and she wasn't looking forward to it.

Every time she had thought about Dr McColl since last night her blood had boiled, sure his intense dislike of the season was to spite her. She'd made no secret of her desire to make this Christmas one to remember but Fraser seemed determined to thwart those efforts at every turn.

Iona told herself it was this battle of wills that made

her react so passionately when she thought of him and nothing to do with whatever frisson she'd imagined when he'd caught her in his arms yesterday. She was no longer the kind of woman who let common sense be overridden by such a romantic cliché. It would take more than being swept off her feet and a handsome face for her to fall for another dominant male. Her sense of self was now defined by her home and her job, not by some fool idea of romance, love and that non-existent fairy-tale ending.

With a deep breath and a sharp knock on the door, she entered Fraser's room out of courtesy rather than a desire to see him for the first time today. In too much of a hurry to waste time on pleasantries, she didn't wait for him to acknowledge her.

'I thought I should give you the heads-up on one of your patients, Marie Gillen. Her baby has tested positive for phenylketonuria.'

There was a slight rise of Fraser's eyebrows before surprise was overtaken by furious typing on the computer keyboard.

'Is this something you've encountered before?' he asked over the sound of the printer whizzing into life.

'Not first hand.' The discovery of rare conditions always brought a range of emotion to the fore, with sympathy for the family at the top of the list. As a medical professional, though, Iona became curious to learn as much as she could to pass on to the parents so they were equipped to deal with whatever challenges were thrown at them. It had to be the same for the GPs who would go on to treat these patients, probably for the rest of their lives.

'Nor me.' Fraser ripped out a handful of printed pages, stapled half together and passed them to Iona, keeping the remainder for himself.

'I'm going to speak to the metabolic unit before I see Mrs Gillen. She'll need a referral straight away.' Since

Marie and her newborn were Iona's patients, she would be the one to oversee the initial handover to the hospital.

'This is some basic info on PKU you can give to her. I'm sure you have it all in hand but it will do us all good to reacquaint ourselves with the challenges ahead.' The way Fraser said it made it sound as though he expected her to make a home visit straight away when she'd intended to wait until she'd spoken to a consultant.

'You know I'm on a half-day? I'm only here until lunchtime because I'm moving house today.' Iona didn't know if he was aware of her time off so she gave him the benefit of the doubt that he wasn't deliberately trying to antagonise her again.

'You can see her first and put the rest of your appointments back. The family need to know and this kind of bombshell is best delivered in person.' When Iona didn't respond immediately, stunned that he was pulling rank on her, Fraser added, 'You know this is a time-sensitive condition and we need to begin treatment as soon as possible.'

She knew he was right and if she hadn't been so caught up in her moving plans she would have suggested the same. As the only midwife at the practice, she didn't have anyone else to delegate to so the responsibility was solely hers to deliver the news to the family. That didn't mean she couldn't be irritated at losing her time off.

The slightest brush of his fingers against hers as he handed her the information started that prickling sensation beneath her skin she'd experienced for the first time last night when he'd held her in his arms just a fraction longer than necessary.

That spark of awareness in Fraser's eyes said he'd felt it too but it only served to annoy Iona more. The GP who'd stolen Christmas was now dousing cold water on the plans for her afternoon off so she shouldn't find anything remotely attractive about him.

'I'm sorry for yesterday but, you know, we have to have a code of conduct in the workplace or all hell would break loose.'

She stared at him, unblinking, wondering if he was trying to justify nixing her time off by blaming her for making a move on *him*. Her cheeks burned all the more when she realised he was talking about her dalliance into interior decorating and she was the only one whose thoughts had strayed elsewhere.

'It's all sorted now. Don't worry about it.' Although Fraser deserved more flak over his over-the-top reaction to a few baubles, it would keep until she'd got over this bout of madness.

'If you need an appointment for me to see Mrs Gillen, let me know and I'll fit her into my schedule.'

There were a lot of things about Fraser that frustrated Iona no end but she couldn't fault his devotion to his patients. Their mutual patients were a shared interest. Somehow that didn't give her any more comfort. Iona greedily snatched at more reasons to dislike him to erase the memory of the tenderness she'd felt in his touch and the desire she'd seen in his eyes when he'd held her close.

In that brief moment she'd understood those defences she'd built up against this man were because she was afraid of liking him too much. She had enough physical and mental scars to be wary of any man, especially the bossy kind, but she worried even that mightn't be enough to save her.

'I'll let you know. I guess moving day will just have to wait.'

Fraser nodded and with her last obligation here taken care of, Iona was able to make her escape from the claustrophobia of these four walls.

There was nothing akin to driving out on the open road, radio blasting and singing along at the top of your voice where no one could hear. Iona loved her job. Sure, it was challenging, the hours long with no discernible time for breaks, but it was rewarding. Not only did she get to accompany these women throughout their pregnancies and sometimes get to welcome their babies into the world herself, she was able to enjoy her independence on a daily basis.

She was free to drive out here in the beautiful Scottish countryside, often travelling for miles between each of her appointments. It gave her that sense of empowerment over her destiny, even though she was still technically an employee.

Her freedom was everything to her after her marriage, during which Andy had practically held her prisoner. She'd been blinded by love in those early days, unable to see how he was slowly isolating her from friends and family, insisting he was the only one she needed in her life. Cut off from anyone who could've helped her, she'd been at the mercy of his temper when it had shown itself. He'd used any excuse to lash out at her—if the dinner had been overcooked or she'd been wearing too much make-up—but towards the end he hadn't even bothered making excuses to beat her it had become so commonplace.

Iona flinched, almost able to feel those blows raining down on her after all this time. It was then she had understood why her mother had endured her own loveless relationship for so long. She'd been worn down, cut off from the outside world with no means to support herself financially when she'd sacrificed everything for her family. It had been Andy's talk of babies and her mother's death that had finally galvanised Iona into action. She could never have brought a child into that toxic atmosphere when she'd grown up in similar herself and had followed the pattern into adulthood.

It had taken death to enable her mother to leave her own

marriage and Iona hadn't been prepared to wait for the same fate. The strength she'd found to walk out on Andy and file for divorce had carried her on to university and to carve out a whole new life for herself.

Placements during her training had seen Iona working in hospitals and birth clinics but that environment had been a conveyor belt of women passing through her hands with no room to get to know them on a personal level. Life as a community midwife gave her much more of an intimate connection, visiting the patients at home and being on hand as they settled into family life.

She took a bite of the pre-packed sandwich she'd bought at the garage on the way back from Mrs Gillen's. Car picnics were Iona's speciality, if not the hearty dinner she'd been hoping to have in her own place tonight. Now all she wanted was to get back and collapse into bed.

It had been a tough day all round with having to deliver baby Gillen's diagnosis. The family had been rocked by the news and it would take some time to come to terms with what it meant for them but they had family close to provide a good support system.

With some liaising with the hospital team she'd managed to arrange a meeting for them tomorrow morning so hopefully that would ease their minds that their son would still live a full and active life with proper guidance.

She'd talked them through the basics of PKU, as outlined in Fraser's printouts, leaving the experts to discuss the day-to-day realities. There had been no need to panic them by overloading them with information when they couldn't do anything until they'd seen the metabolic consultant and dietician who'd be overseeing the treatment.

The circumstances, however, dictated Iona had stayed with the family much longer than she'd anticipated and she'd been forced to push the rest of her appointments back. It wasn't something she was happy doing to people waiting in for her but given the cold weather her patients had assured her they'd no intention of venturing outside today. She didn't blame them. Given half a chance, she'd have stayed indoors with a mug of hot chocolate and a cheesy Christmas film on the TV.

Of course, the extra time had meant not only had she missed out on her afternoon off but the surgery would likely be closed by now and she'd wanted to stop by to grab a few things for tomorrow.

After eight months in the village Iona knew the area pretty well but in the dark, with the first flurry of snow visible in the car headlights, these remote roads were daunting, to say the least. When she saw the lights on at the clinic ahead she breathed a sigh of relief that she'd made it back in one piece and she could stock up on supplies for tomorrow's excursions.

It would be an early start tomorrow again in order to keep up to date with all of her patients and paperwork. Being a midwife required stamina and not for the first time she was glad she didn't have to go home and go straight into wife and mother mode to keep others happy. As soon as she was done here she could go home and slip into the guise of knackered singleton guilt-free.

'Hello. It's Iona. Can you let me in?' She rapped on the clinic window, hoping whoever was here, cleaning or catching up on last-minute paperwork, would open up.

'I hope you're not expecting overtime.' Fraser's dour tone almost tipped her over the edge into a rant about putting her patients above financial gain and her own plans, until she saw the tease playing on his lips. In her exhausted state Iona wasn't sure she was prepared to deal with the sight.

'I just want to restock with supplies for tomorrow morning.' Iona didn't rise to the bait, not willing to prolong her working day any longer than necessary. With his large frame filling the doorway, she chose to duck under his arm as he held the door open, rather than take the chance of touching him again by pushing past.

'How is Mrs Gillen?' Unable to take the hint that she didn't want him near her, Fraser followed her into the stockroom. Iona should've known he'd want a full account to analyse if she'd handled the situation correctly, no doubt concerned he'd be the one to pick up the pieces if Marie fell apart.

'Shocked, obviously, but reasonably calm. I passed on the printouts you provided.' He could give himself a pat on the back that he'd participated in some way if that's what he was interested in.

'Good. Good. Would you like me to make an emergency appointment to discuss any concerns with her?' With his arms folded and resting casually against the shelves, Fraser left scant breathing space in the small room. There really was no reason for them both to be crammed in here so Iona forced her way past into the corridor so she wasn't suffocated by his spicy aftershave.

'No, I've made arrangements for her at the metabolic unit. The consultant and dietician will take over from here.' She doubted he'd be one hundred percent happy about being out of the loop but there were areas even out of his expertise.

'They know best,' he conceded politely.

'How come you're here so late?' Usually you could set your watch by Fraser, who tried to keep office hours when he wasn't on call. He'd never have made it as a midwife.

The idea of him in blue scrubs, tootling around the countryside in her small car, made her grin and she had to turn away so he wouldn't see her amusement.

'I thought I'd swot up on PKU while I was waiting for you.'

The admission made her do an about-turn. 'Me? What on earth for?'

Their contretemps over the decorations immediately sprang to mind, along with that back-of-the-neck tingling sensation. Her pulse apparently thought she was in a sprint and other parts of her were reminding her it had been a long time since she'd been with a man and she should simply acknowledge this growing attraction for her colleague. If the opportunity arose to get close again, she couldn't be certain common sense would get any say in the matter when her hormones were currently doing all the talking.

'I thought you might need help moving in.' The expression on Fraser's face displayed concern rather than an intention to seduce her. He was the innocent party in the lurid fantasies her overtired mind insisted on conjuring up.

'I'll just have to reschedule for the next time I'm free. Whenever that might be.' Her need for sleep now was more vital than assuaging Fraser's apparent guilt that she'd been held up and she wished she'd never broached the subject with him. It put her in a no-win situation. Saying no to him wasn't going to help their already strained relationship but letting him trespass into her private life wasn't going to be comfortable for either of them.

'Call it my apology for yesterday. I could've handled things better.' Hands in pockets, he gave a shrug and appeared even less of a tyrant than ever. None of that was helping Iona maintain that wall of steel she tried to surround herself with at the merest hint of a too-alpha male. Sincere apologies and taking responsibility for anything weren't traits often associated with such domineering personalities. She should know.

On this occasion Iona had to consider the possibility she might have been mistaken in her assessment of Fraser McColl. Then she could stop being so hard on herself for being drawn to him. Unfortunately this humble side of him decreed a compromise on her part lest she become the sort of obstinate-to-a-fault twit she despised.

'Me too. I should've asked before I did my sugar-plum fairy act. I got a bit carried away.'

'Really? I hadn't noticed.' There was that grin again and Iona wondered if it was reserved for the privileged few or it only made appearances out of working hours. It was unnerving that she even wanted to know what her relevance was to the rare sighting.

'It's my first Christmas in my own home, free from demanding family members, messy flatmates and fussy co-workers. Excuse me for being a tad over-excited.' It spoke volumes that the first purchases for her new place had been an abundance of Christmas paraphernalia instead of essential household appliances.

'I can't say I understand the need for the fuss but each to their own as long as it doesn't leak onto the premises again.' Fraser verbally slapped the back of her hand but she'd had much worse from other men she'd inadvertently ticked off in the past.

'What do you have against Christmas anyway?' Since they appeared to have embarked on a truce, Iona thought it best to find out as much as she could about the elusive doctor before the clock chimed and he transformed back into his monstrous alter-ego.

She could see the inner struggle he was having as to whether or not to share the reasons behind his anti-Christmas stance in his hesitation to reply. He was watching her as though judging if she was trustworthy enough to keep his secrets.

Eventually Fraser sighed and said, 'My mother died on Christmas Eve. I was six when they first discovered she had breast cancer. I haven't really celebrated since, packed off out of the way to boarding school when she first became ill. Come to think of it, I don't remember ever celebrating even before I associated her death with Christmas. It's just not a point in my life I'm keen to relive every year.'

The heartfelt explanation shook Iona to her core—she had never expected such an honest and bleak insight into his background. As someone whose job was all about families and protecting young children, it was only natural Fraser's story should get her choked up. She knew how traumatic it was to lose a mother but at such a young age he must've suffered dreadfully.

It explained a lot about his negative outlook on the season and she winced at how tactless her actions now seemed with hindsight. The shock of seeing those decorations would've brought those painful memories flooding back to him and it was no wonder he'd been angry at her. She was sorry that he'd been denied the joy in sharing Christmas with family but she didn't want to pry too far into his personal life and jeopardise their ceasefire. It wasn't as though she was keen to discuss Christmases gone by either.

'I understand that and I'm really sorry for your loss but if you ever need someone to sprinkle a little Christmas magic, you know where to find me.' It wasn't a serious offer when it was probably too late to change his opinion on the subject but she did manage to get him to smile.

'I certainly do but don't let my hang-ups encroach on your obvious enthusiasm. You're perfectly entitled to celebrate however you choose, in your personal life.'

'It is a big deal for me this year,' Iona said apologetically, understanding his point of view but also determined to go all out for herself.

'In that case, we should start with getting you moved in properly.' Fraser turned off the lights and ushered her towards the door so he could set the alarm.

Ready or not, her new best friend was coming home with her for the night.

CHAPTER THREE

'LET ME GET that for you.' Fraser made a grab for the door while balancing a heavy cardboard box in his other hand.

'It's fine. I can manage.' Iona, who could barely be seen over the top of the stacked boxes in her arms, insisted on doing it herself.

'No problem.' He took a step back so she wouldn't think he was trying to crowd her. Iona was so independent Fraser always felt he was in her way somehow, even though she would never have managed to move all of this on her own.

None of this had been in his plans tonight. He had, instead, been anticipating another quiet night in with nothing but the clock chimes echoing through the house to disturb him. It had been his guilty conscience preventing him from walking away from the whole situation when he'd heard from other staff members how excited she'd been about moving in tonight.

Iona nudged the door open with her bottom but he wasn't sure how they were going to manoeuvre her belongings up the narrow staircase leading to the flat above the shop.

'Sorry. I didn't mean to snap. It's just…this is a milestone for me.' The apology was as much of a surprise as the tears he could see making her eyes shine like glossy chocolate. It was clearly an emotional moment for her and probably for more than the reasons she'd given him. He'd experienced something similar when he'd taken over the family home after his father had passed away, believing it was going to be the start of his new life with a wife and children, surrounded by love for the first time. Before then, being on his own had been something he'd simply taken for granted because he didn't remember life before it.

Even if he hadn't had his hands full, Iona didn't give him a chance to pry any further as she made her way upstairs. Clearly the sharing of personal information was only coming from one direction tonight. Fraser had surprised himself by telling her about his mother's death. It wasn't something he usually told people and certainly not those he had trouble getting along with. However, he did want to explain his behaviour surrounding the Christmas issue so she wouldn't hate him too much. Since she hadn't slammed the door on him, Fraser had assumed he'd made the right move.

He'd kept finding excuses to stay behind at the surgery tonight—paperwork, the weather, waiting for news on the Gillens—but as soon as Iona had arrived he'd realised he'd been waiting to see her again so he could make it up to her for spoiling her plans. He had been sure she would come back to make preparations for the next working day and he suspected his overtime had been driven partially by curiosity over that frisson between them last night. It had definitely been attraction on his part, unexpected and somewhat inconvenient since they were co-workers and not harmonious ones at that.

Wandering the empty corridors of his family home, Fraser had little else to focus on other than his work and now that it had become entangled in his personal life it was impossible not to spend the night thinking about Iona.

He didn't know what he'd expected to come of seeing her after hours but he certainly hadn't imagined going home with her. With their history he'd never thought she'd actually agree to let him help.

It wasn't immediately obvious if her concession was for purely practical reasons or if she, too, was keen to explore that new chemistry between them. He wasn't about to ask when any possible answer was sure to unsettle him more. A dalliance with a colleague was totally out of the question, too disruptive, too close to home, and it had disaster written all over it. He couldn't afford to have his love life screwing things up at work when he was just beginning to get things the way he wanted.

'I know what you're thinking.'

Fraser nearly dropped Iona's belongings at being caught having inappropriate thoughts about her.

'What's that?' He aimed for a neutral 'I have no idea what you're talking about' tone as he stacked his box on top of the ones she'd positioned on the floor. There was still a car full of bric-a-brac outside but he reckoned he could unload it into the hall in double-quick time if he incurred her wrath.

'Why would I leave a pretty chocolate-box cottage for this only a few days before Christmas?'

Once it became clear his thoughts remained private, Fraser deemed it safe to engage in conversation again. 'It's none of my business.'

Since she'd pointed it out, the contrast between the homely bungalow he'd helped her empty to come to this shell of an apartment did raise questions.

'I mean, Mrs Dunlop said I was welcome to stay as my rent is paid up until the New Year.'

'But you're excited about having your own place? I think you mentioned that.' Fraser could tell how happy Iona was. Her smile was warm enough to heat the whole building—which was just as well because he doubted the central heating had been on since the last tenant had vacated the property.

Personally, Fraser couldn't see the attraction but, given how Iona had no qualms about making her mark at the surgery, he was certain she'd quickly make it a home. As soon as she bought some furniture. Unless this was one of those futuristic, space-saving apartments where the fixtures and fittings popped up from the floor at the touch of a button, she really didn't have any furniture of note.

Iona's quirks were in danger of bringing Fraser out in hives, her inability to plan ahead making him itch. When he'd transferred his stuff from his bachelor pad to the family home he'd allocated a specific timescale for completion, with all his things boxed and labelled accordingly for the removal company. Iona had randomly chucked things into cardboard boxes and bin liners with no forethought given to how she expected to find anything again. Even if she hadn't got caught up at work, there was no way she'd have managed to get things in order in the space of one afternoon.

'I do have a bed, well, a mattress, and there's a kettle here somewhere.' She began rifling through everything, unwrapping the contents until the floorboards were littered with bits of newspaper and kitchen paraphernalia.

'I'll go and bring the rest in.' Fraser couldn't stand back and watch this level of chaos without wanting to fix it. Something he knew Iona wouldn't appreciate. This wasn't his mess or responsibility and he had to get used to the fact Iona had chosen to live this way.

By the time he'd lugged the rest of her trash chic luggage into the flat Iona had moved into the kitchen. It would be generous to call the space open-plan, it was more in keeping with a student bedsit or, in its current state, a squat.

He shuddered as he set the bags down in the one space he could find amongst the mess she'd already created.

'If that's everything, I'll head home.' Back to his pristine house, which didn't look as though it had just been burgled.

'Look what I found!' Ignoring his plea to be released back into civilised society, Iona held up the elusive kettle and two mismatched mugs.

'Great,' Fraser muttered through clenched teeth, accepting his fate. It wouldn't help relations between them if he declined her hospitality when she was trying to be friendly.

'For a job well done.' Iona clinked her mug to his once she'd completed her task, oblivious to his discomfort in the corduroy beanbag serving as his seat during their tea break. The chipped cartoon cat mug he was drinking from was a world away from his mother's fine china he'd become accustomed to.

'So, er, what are your plans for the place?' The old outhouse, long forgotten somewhere on the family estate, was more inviting than these four bare walls, yet Iona was so pleased with it Fraser wondered what kind of place she was used to.

Iona shrugged and slurped her tea. 'I'll get some paint to freshen it up a bit for Christmas and I'll pick up whatever bits and pieces I need along the way.'

Fraser snorted in disbelief at her *laissez-faire* attitude to being a homeowner. For someone so fastidious about her work and keeping track of her patients, Iona was very blasé about her own personal life.

'We're very different creatures, you and I.' Fraser supposed she would be as ill at ease with his set-up—with the family heirlooms giving it that look-but-don't-touch vibe that made people hover nervously—as he was here.

'I thought we'd figured that out a long time ago.' She

was teasing, even though there'd been nothing funny about their previous arguments.

'We've had our moments.' This insight into Iona's chaotic world, such a contrast to the one Fraser had created around himself, made sense of their feisty exchanges. They were completely different people and living up to that adage about opposites. Last night they'd finally recognised the attraction even if they hadn't acted on it.

Somewhere across the room Iona cleared her throat and he knew her mind had ventured into the same dangerous territory as his.

Fraser drained the last of his tea. He'd become too comfortable in Iona's company, if not her new dwelling. 'Time to go.'

'Thanks again for all your help.'

He struggled to clamber out of the shape-shifting cushion trying to swallow him whole, which didn't help the growing sense of panic clawing at his chest. He had to get away from here, be somewhere safe and orderly where he wouldn't be ambushed by the furnishings or unexpected emotions.

'Perhaps I'll start my purchases with a chair or two.' Iona came to his aid, holding out her hand to hoist him out of the man trap.

'Not on my account,' Fraser insisted. He had no intention of coming back here and certainly not to relive those distracting feelings he kept experiencing around her. If only he'd stuck to his schedule, all of this could have been avoided. This kind of havoc was exactly what happened when he didn't abide by his own rules.

'You never know who's going to drop in and, as I've just witnessed, not everyone's used to slumming it on beanbags.' Unlike his, Iona's place was the sort people would be dropping into whenever the notion took them. She wasn't the type to be governed by social etiquette outside work, which made her home so much more appealing than the formal invitation one would require to gain admittance to his. Fraser couldn't remember the last time he'd even had a house guest but that isolation was part of the charm as far as he was concerned.

Fraser negotiated his way through the detritus on the floor, waved goodbye at the door, but for the entire journey home he couldn't help worrying on Iona's behalf about her lack of preparation for the move. Neither could he put out the thought of the contents of his own apartment sitting in storage now he had no use for them. Iona was so pleased with so little but she really deserved better, and with a small effort on his part he could provide it for her *and* have her think of him a tad more fondly. He didn't know why her acceptance had suddenly become important to him but it might have had something to do with her smiling at him instead of the usual scowl he elicited.

It warmed him on the inside, reaching parts of him he'd thought frozen in time along with the contents of his family home.

Even though he was worn out after his impulsive house removal, he knew he'd be returning to that compact residence before the night was over. Whatever spell had been cast on him the minute he'd taken Iona in his arms Fraser couldn't seem to stay away from her and that definitely didn't fit in with his plans for a carefully organised life.

Iona sank back into her bubble bath and closed her eyes. This was just what she needed after such a fraught day. Okay, so she'd had to wait for a while for the hot water to come through but like everything else wrong in the flat she was happy to put up with it when she was now the proud owner of all she surveyed.

A secret smile played across her lips as she thought of Fraser's reaction on seeing the place. The outright horror on his face had been comical and she'd admit to intentionally pushing his buttons by leaving everything lying around to see if he'd try to tidy her up outside work. Iona knew he preferred everything spick and span as he was forever rearranging things in the waiting room, but since he'd insisted on stepping into her personal life, this was her way of marking her territory, creating a boundary. There was a chance she'd also been trying to rile him so he would overstep the mark and criticise her so she could stop thinking of him as anything other than her tyrannical boss.

To his credit, he hadn't risen to the bait, proving there was some restraint and positive qualities behind his fussy, bossy exterior He'd been generous with his time and support for her tonight and, coupled with yesterday's revelation that her urges towards him weren't only of a violent nature, she was losing track of the reasons to give him a wide berth. At least he'd made it clear he wasn't in a hurry to come back any time soon so she wouldn't have to worry too much over the consequences of inviting another man into her life.

It was easy to recall the feel of Fraser's hands, strong and capable as he'd cradled her after the fall, and imagine how they might feel on different parts of her body. Iona soaped a flannel up her arms and across her chest, startled that her thoughts of Fraser had turned so…carnal.

She let out a groan and covered her face with the cloth. It wasn't as though she'd become a nun on leaving her abusive ex but she'd put her career ahead of any notions of settling down again after being bitten, and a relationship of any kind had been the furthest thing from her mind. As far as she'd discovered, they only brought pain and heartache to everyone involved and she'd had enough of that to know she was better off unattached.

Now she'd settled into her position here and got her foot on the property ladder, it seemed her neglected libido was making a bid for freedom too. Its untimely reappearance around a man with the uncanny knack of riling her temper was entirely inconvenient—a weakness in the armour she'd built around herself since her reinvention. This warrior queen no longer needed anyone to give her life meaning.

Iona ducked her head under the suds, letting the hot water envelop her whole body in a warm hug. It had obviously been way too long since she'd enjoyed the physical benefits of a relationship of any description when her mind was dragging her towards that riptide with the potential to pull her back under.

In her watery cocoon Iona thought she could feel a dull vibration coming from somewhere beneath the flat. She sat upright, listening to the rhythmic drip, drip, drip of the tap, which almost lulled her back down into the depths of soapy luxury until the shrill ring of the doorbell and more thumping noises downstairs prompted her to action. Someone was desperate for her attention.

'I'm coming!' she yelled, pulling on her dressing gown with no heed to the water sluicing onto the bathroom floor. There was no time to dry or dress if she was to get to the door before they left so she simply belted the robe around her naked body to protect her modesty.

Fraser was the last person she expected to find on her doorstep.

'What's wrong? Did you forget something?' She couldn't think of any other reason that would have brought him back again so soon.

'No. I…er…thought you could use these.' He glanced over his shoulder towards the stack of chairs Iona hadn't noticed currently blocking the path.

'And they couldn't wait until tomorrow?' Although it was a nice gesture, it hadn't warranted an immediate return visit tonight. The impulsive act was so out of character she was thrown by his possible motive. Was this intended to impress her or an attempt to impose his authority in all areas of her life?

Iona folded her arms and did her best to make Fraser realise she wasn't impressed that he'd interrupted her 'me' time for the sake of a couple of chairs so he wouldn't get used to the idea of dropping in at will. It did the trick as he grimaced and gave her his best game-show-host impression in trying to sell her the quality of his wares with a flick of his hands.

'I couldn't bear to think of you here in this empty flat when I have a load of furniture sitting in storage.' He gestured to the vehicle behind him, having apparently exchanged the practical car he drove to work for a gas-guzzling four-by-four packed with other household goods.

'Really? This has absolutely nothing to do with you trying to *fix* me? I know you, Fraser, and how much my empty apartment was probably keeping you from sleeping.' Her cynical eyebrow took on a mind of its own as she searched for a dark ulterior motive behind the selfless offer. He'd made it obvious he had issues with her laid-back approach to her interior décor but she hadn't realised it was to the extent he'd empty the contents of his home to spruce hers up.

'Sorry. I was trying to do you a favour. I probably should've asked first.' Fraser took a step back, shoulders slumped with such dejection Iona may as well have told him never to darken her doorstep again. It was a trick she'd seen her ex use time and again to garner her sympathy and she'd always fallen for it, believing she'd been judging him too harshly and accepting an apology for whatever misdeed he'd committed against her. Only for him to exploit that weakness, lull her back into a false sense of security and strike even harder next time around.

She was less trusting these days but she had absolutely no obligation to Fraser so if he did overstep the mark in any way, she wouldn't hesitate in bouncing him back down the path.

'I'm not dressed for company, or furniture delivery.' Standing here in the cold, face to face with the subject of her recent fantasies, made her aware that she was clad only in a layer of terry towelling.

'No problem. If you want to put some clothes on, I can bring the stuff inside for you then I'll get out of your hair.' There certainly didn't appear to be any sign of anything untoward going on behind his earnest expression and she could use the items he was offering. This would be no run-of-the-mill second-hand furniture either, having probably been vacuum packed in plastic wrap to prevent it being spoiled.

'If you insist.' She left the door open and scarpered back upstairs to put some clothes on. Things were awkward enough without hanging around him semi-naked and partially aroused.

Iona did take her time getting ready, going as far as drying her hair before venturing out of her bedroom again. Fraser deserved a hard time for trying to organise her life for her so she let him sweat for a while. Literally.

When she walked back into the living room he was breathing heavily, the sleeves of his once pristine shirt now rolled up and her flat looking as though someone actually lived in it.

Not only had he carted all the heavy furniture up a flight of stairs single-handed, he'd arranged it all and tidied up the mess she'd left on the floor earlier.

'You really didn't have to do this,' Iona protested, tightening her grip on that theory Fraser was only doing it to exert some control over her. Yet, amongst the seats and the table he'd set up, there was also a small electric fire and a television solely provided for her comfort and not any obvious ulterior motive. Perhaps he deserved some credit for his thoughtfulness but that meant accepting she'd been on his mind tonight too and she certainly didn't want to contemplate the implications of that.

'I wanted to,' Fraser said simply, and continued unpacking a bag onto her kitchen worktop.

'What are you doing?' As far as she was aware, she was the only one named on the mortgage and she hadn't advertised for a lodger but here he was, making himself at home.

'I didn't think you'd had time to do a shop so I picked up a few essentials for you on the way over.'

Bread, bacon, butter, eggs, milk and a huge chocolate bar lined the counter as though he knew her shopping list off by heart. Although he was providing the means to christen her new home with all her favourites, Iona didn't want him to think she was a pushover, someone who could be trained with titbits of chocolate. She was in charge of her life now and didn't need anyone making decisions on her behalf. It would be easy to take all his efforts at face value, and as much as she wanted to believe he only had the purest of intentions at heart she had to protect herself by assuming the worst. Andy had made it impossible for her to trust anyone, especially handsome men who seemed too good to be true.

'You really didn't have to. I'm quite capable of going to the shop myself, thank you.'

'I know. I just thought—I wanted you to feel more at home. Sorry.' He started to pack the groceries back into the bag and the waver in his confidence about being there had guilt gnawing at Iona's insides that she'd got him wrong. Perhaps Fraser *was* simply trying to do something nice for her after all. Learning to trust new people was a long and difficult journey every time, no matter how hard she wanted to speed up the process.

'No, it's okay. Leave them.' Iona reached out and touched his hand to get him to stop and show him the gifts were appreciated. His sharp intake of breath and her reluctance to move back out of his personal space drew them back into that fizzing awareness of attraction to one another.

This thing between them was nothing either of them could control but she knew Fraser didn't want to act on it any more than she did. They were complete opposites; they'd drive each other crazy.

Every nerve ending in her body was drawing Iona closer, telling her to submit once and for all. Yet, with Fraser refusing to succumb too, she held her ground. A rejection now would be humiliating every day for the rest of her working life here. If he declined her advances now, it would give him the perfect excuse to undermine her the next time they clashed at the clinic, blaming her hurt feelings for her next bout of stubbornness. A risk she wasn't willing to take if it could jeopardise any future decisions regarding her patients' welfare.

Eventually Iona forced herself to return to the less dangerous task of putting the groceries away in the cupboards.

'How did you come to have so much spare furniture?' She kept her tone casual, even though her heart was pounding with as much adrenaline and arousal as if they had kissed because she'd imagined it so vividly.

There were a few beats before she heard Fraser move away. As though it had taken him that time to shake himself out of the daze too. 'My dad died a couple of years ago and I inherited the family home. I sold my apartment and moved back but I haven't decided if it's what I want on a permanent basis.'

Keeping hold of the contents of his place if he'd sold it didn't make much sense to Iona, but she understood the death of a parent was such an emotional upheaval it brought about huge life changes. It had been her mother's death that had prompted her to strike out on her own regardless of not having anywhere to go or anyone to help her.

'Sorry for your loss.' It was a sentiment she'd heard so often herself yet seemed so inadequate when it passed from her own lips. Those four words could never hope to comfort someone who'd suffered such a devastating event. She'd never known how to respond to it either. It wasn't the done thing to burst into tears or go off on a rant about how unfair it was so she'd learned to graciously nod and thank people for their condolences.

'We weren't really close. Not since Mum died. Or ever, really.' Fraser was disarmingly frank about his relationship with his father and Iona was shocked to discover they had more in common than either of them had realised.

'I know the feeling. It's hard to bond with a parent in those circumstances. Almost as though you're being forced into a relationship you never had because the one you were closest to has gone for ever.' In those early days after her mother's death Iona had done and said all the right things expected of a dutiful daughter trying to make sure her dad wouldn't feel the loss as acutely as she did, filling that role of caregiver left empty by the woman who'd sacrificed everything for her family. None of it had come naturally and she had soon come to realise it had been fear and grief fuelling her actions, not love. She'd rather be alone than submit to another man's whim again.

Fraser was such a strong, confident individual she didn't imagine he'd been in quite the same position with his family but it would explain that frostiness he exuded at times. She knew she'd erected a lot of barriers to keep herself safe when she'd moved away. It had taken a lot of time to make herself accessible to people again, and only because she'd wanted to work in such a people-friendly environment. She was still working on the walls she'd barricaded around her heart, which weren't dismantled so easily. She wasn't sure she'd ever be ready for them to come down again.

Fraser's loss and the anger and sorrow that surely had been part of that were relatively recent and raw. Something he would have to work hard to get past. It wasn't so unbelievable that it formed part of the reason he hadn't moved in for that kiss when the opportunity had arisen. That lessened the sting slightly but also flashed more warning lights that this complex man was the last one she should set her cap at.

'I can't say I was really any closer to my mother but it's all in the past. We're supposed to be celebrating your future.' Fraser smiled but there was a sadness behind it that touched her heart so deeply she couldn't tell if she wanted to reach out and hug him or rip off his clothes.

His decision to move back to the family home rather than stay in his own place seemed all the more bizarre if it held such dark memories for him. Given the same opportunity, she'd prefer to slum it in her Borrowers-sized flat than move back to a house echoing with tears of the past. A clean break was the only way to leave those ghosts behind.

'You didn't think about selling up?' A senior partner in a thriving GP practice with no discernible dependants that Iona knew of should've had the means to live wherever he wanted. Unless he had some debilitating addiction syphoning off his pay packet but she couldn't picture Fraser with any vices that would have seen him spiralling into that kind of desperation.

'It—it's complicated. Walking away isn't really an option, being the last of the McColls.'

She'd heard the rumours that he came from a wealthy background so there was a chance his father had written a clause into his will that Fraser would only inherit if he remained in situ. The kind of emotional manipulation that made it difficult to leave an abusive relationship. Including one from beyond the grave, it would seem.

Iona was lucky that she'd had her mother in her corner, trying to provide some sort of stability, when her father had made no attempt to hide the fact he'd rather have been anywhere than at home with his family. If both of her parents had been demanding and continually messing with her head, she would never have survived this far.

'What about you? No other family or friends nearby who could help you out?' Fraser turned his back on her to go and play with the heater he'd provided, an orange glow flickering in the fake fire screen at the touch of a switch providing a cosier atmosphere already.

'I see a lot of my ex-patients but they've got young families to take care of. Then there's Katherine, but she's not in any condition to do anything but waddle these days.' Katherine was her recently widowed, pregnant colleague currently on maternity leave and probably Iona's only real friend here. She didn't mind her social calendar being pretty much empty when this was supposed to be her new start away from the demands everyone else put on her time.

'I meant outside work.' Given Fraser's usual gruff demeanour, it was difficult to picture a queue of people lined up at his door, waiting to take him out for a night on the town either, so this interest in her out-of-hours activities seemed unnecessarily intrusive.

'I'm a long way from home and, as you know, our line of work can be very demanding. It's not a typical nine-to-five job. Colleagues, and patients to some extent, are my friends.' Iona became so involved with the families it was impossible to sever ties completely and she often received calls in the middle of the night, asking for advice. There wasn't space for her to be lonely and she happened to enjoy her own company. Having anyone in her home, especially of the male variety, was a novelty and not something she wanted to get used to.

'Now you're in the centre of the village I'm sure you'll get to know everyone very well.'

Iona got the impression he was encouraging her to socialise to get himself off the hook from having to bail her out again. Which wasn't a bad idea if it limited those sparky moments between them, although he'd been a great help tonight. She couldn't pinpoint the exact moment when they'd moved from foes to making cow eyes at each other, or which one was more damaging to her well-being. Particularly when she didn't want him to leave.

This was one of those occasions when Fraser was grateful for his bolthole in the hills. There had been many times when he was on call or the roads were treacherous with snow and ice that his location was a nuisance. Tonight, however, it would be good to put some distance between him and Iona.

They'd become too close, too soon, in the space of twenty-four hours for him to be comfortable. Not that the effort of the drive had put him off coming over for a second time tonight. The sight of Iona fresh out of the shower, hair wet and wearing nothing but a robe, had made the trip worth it. He'd fallen over himself to install his long-neglected furniture, which he'd retrieved from the converted barn at the back of the main house.

If he got her set up tonight, spread the word that she'd moved into the centre of the village and needed a few friendly faces to come and welcome her, he'd have no more excuses to make himself available.

He crouched down by the heater to demonstrate and relay instructions so there was no confusion on how to operate it and no need for him to worry about her shivering here.

'It's very straightforward. This is the on switch—'

'And, let me guess, this turns it on?' Iona knelt beside him, their thighs almost touching as she made fun of him.

They were back to where all this trouble had started, locked in that lustful gaze, battling between their libidos and common sense, desire pulling them closer than the world's strongest magnets, their mouths and restraint venturing into the danger zone.

That red-blooded male trapped inside the body of a man described by his ex as 'too buttoned-up to love' was screaming out to kiss her. Well, for once Fraser wasn't going to hold back and would be true to himself and his feelings instead. If that's what it took to be with Iona, he was willing to change from the stuffed shirt he had a tendency to be.

He kissed her. Hard.

Her hands cupped his face and she returned the kiss with equal abandon.

Fraser couldn't remember the last time he'd felt so alive, so aware of his every breath, every beat of his heart, quickening with each flick of her tongue against his. If this was what he'd been missing out on by playing by the rules all this time, he'd be throwing the etiquette book right out the window.

Iona fell back onto the floor, bringing him with her until he was splayed across her body, every soft curve of her lush body hardening his. He wanted her to the point where nothing else mattered except exploring this walk on the wild side with her.

Somewhere in the depths of his hormonally dazed brain Fraser registered her hands pushing against his chest and he wasn't so far gone he'd ignore any hesitation on her part. He immediately rolled away and apologised.

'I'm so sorry. I thought you wanted this too.' He'd never forgive himself if he'd made an unwanted advance.

Iona sat up looking every bit as dazed and confused as he was about what had just happened. Or had almost happened. 'I do, I did, but let's be honest, this isn't me and I'm fairly certain this isn't you. Thanks for your help with everything but I think we should call it a night. We have work in the morning.'

She got to her feet and headed towards the door without looking back at him, leaving Fraser in no doubt that she wanted him to leave now so they could revert back to solely work colleagues tomorrow. He didn't blame her when he was at a loss to explain what had come over him other than pure lust. That didn't make the rebuff any easier to take when he'd put himself out there in a way he hadn't done in a long time. If only he could rewind the clock back to earlier in the night when he'd first left the premises and avoided taking another blow to his confidence and their working relationship! Then he wouldn't be returning home with an even worse opinion of himself than if he hadn't tried to help her.

The irony of this was, of course, that Fraser was trying to be himself, acting completely on impulse without moderating himself as he usually did, or trying to be the person he imagined people wanted him to be.

Yet Iona had rejected him just the way Caroline had when she too had accused him of not being true to himself. Perhaps he simply had to face facts. There was no one willing to love him for who he was, or who he tried to be for them.

CHAPTER FOUR

IONA WAS LOATH to leave her new flat the next morning, wishing she had some time off to fully immerse herself in unpacking. The task itself wouldn't take her more than a couple of hours but she could spread that out to last a full day with a chance to binge-watch some of the DVD box sets she had waiting for her.

Since she'd decided to keep her days off for the Christmas period Iona had to carry on her working day as usual and save her solo housewarming party for then.

Her unusual reluctance to get to work might also have had something to do with Fraser's unexpected late-night visit and their nocturnal shenanigans.

She'd finally conceded that his attempt to furnish her flat had been thoughtful, generous and more than appreciated, but it was the re-ignition of that heat between them that had made the night especially unforgettable. Every time she thought of Fraser now, her blood boiled for more than their clash over the Christmas decorations in the clinic. It wasn't a secret they had a clash of personalities but who knew it had been the build-up of such immense sexual tension between them? That kiss, and her reaction to it, had been as much as a surprise as the wild passion Fraser had apparently been hiding under his buttoned-up shirt.

A fluttery sensation started in the pit of her stomach and

quickly spread throughout the rest of her body as she recalled the intensity with which they'd dived on each other. As though they'd tired of pretending the chemistry didn't exist and had abandoned themselves to it instead. Desire for Fraser had hit Iona so hard it had literally knocked her off her feet and she could have given herself completely to him at that moment.

Their time together last night proved that first encounter hadn't been a one-off and it scared her half to death. Iona wasn't so damaged by her ex that she believed every man who crossed her path was going to physically abuse her but she remembered how it was to have to constantly think about the other person in a relationship—their moods, their feelings, their needs—and how exhausted it made her. There was little joy in it for her and on balance there was more benefit for her to remain single.

Although she couldn't shake off the knowledge that chemistry between them would be equally as explosive in the bedroom as it was in the workplace. Fraser's kiss alone had had more heat and passion than she'd experienced in her marriage or any college dalliances since but she wasn't going to get burned again. This was the same man who liked to 'take an interest' in her patients, as he put it, whereas she thought of it more as checking up on her. Enough reason for her to give him a wide berth.

If she ever got involved with another man it would have to be with someone who was content to let her be herself, without a desire to bend her to his will. Fraser McColl would never settle until she'd come to heel. The food and furniture delivery was proof enough he was incapable of letting her run her own life without his interference.

Going into the surgery this morning, Iona's stomach was tied in knots wondering how he'd respond to her after her epic rejection and if his bruised ego would make life more difficult for her at the clinic.

'Morning, Victoria,' she called to the receptionist, not stopping for her usual chat in the hope she would manage to dodge Fraser on her way through the clinic.

She knew he was there on the discovery of his labelled, neatly stacked plastic containers in the communal staff fridge. The sight always gave her the urge to mess up his arrangement out of sheer badness. This morning, however, she resisted targeting the regimented meals and fruit snacks since he had gone out of his way to help her before things had spiralled spectacularly out of control.

This morning she had her antenatal clinic so it wasn't unheard of for her to run into Fraser at some point, or indeed consult on the treatment of mutual patients. On walking past his room, she noticed the door was firmly closed, a sign he didn't want to be disturbed by anyone. Fraser didn't normally shut himself off from the outside world until his first patient of the day had taken a seat. It was going to be awkward facing each other after that wanton display they'd put on in her living room but they'd have to get over it when they still had to work together. Regardless of how difficult it was going to be to put the thought of that spine-tingling kiss to the back of her mind.

Her day was taken up with the usual pre-pregnancy checks keeping her too busy to dwell on what was going on behind Dr McColl's closed door. It wasn't her business to know what was going on in his head but it was her job to be professional and supportive to every mum-to-be and make sure her ladies and their babies were progressing as they should.

'Roughly how often do you feel the baby move?'

'Have you given any thought to breast-feeding?'

'How are you feeling generally?'

There'd been no complications or referrals so far today

so that meant she'd get out for her home visits on schedule. There was no better way to leave Fraser and that lapse in judgement behind than to get onto the open road and put the vast rural Scottish countryside between them. At least her next patient was bound to close her clinic on a high.

'Katherine!' Iona rushed to give the heavily pregnant woman a hug, or as close to it as her protruding round belly would allow.

'Having a rough day or are you just happy to see me?' Katherine backed herself into the nearest chair and sat down with all the grace of a reversing truck, leaving her other two charges hovering nervously at either side of her.

Hamish and Poppy were too old to be pacified with the box of toddler toys here to entertain the children who often accompanied their mothers, yet were too young to be left unattended in the waiting room for the duration of this appointment.

'Both.' Iona helped Katherine with the shoes she was struggling to take off and pulled a couple of extra chairs over for the little ones.

Iona handed out the lollipops she kept for restless children and improvised some art supplies with printer paper and whatever pens and pencils she had lying around in order to keep their minds and hands occupied so she could have a proper discussion with their mum. Once they were ensconced at her desk she helped Katherine up onto the bed and pulled the curtain partially around her for at least the illusion of privacy.

'Sorry. They've been playing up this morning and I didn't want to send them to school only to get a phone call to drive back and collect them again. They're complaining about tummyache, but as you can see...' Katherine indicated the empty lolly wrappers and the hands dipping into the jar for seconds '...it comes and goes. I think they're just missing their dad.'

'It's only natural.'

Katherine was one of their own, a practice nurse at the clinic who'd taken Iona under her wing when she'd started. The excitement over her new pregnancy had been matched with that of sharing it with her new friend.

Neither of them had expected she'd lose her husband so early to brain cancer only weeks after his diagnosis. The loss and grief had caused Iona to keep a close eye on Katherine, providing a shoulder to cry on and her mobile number for whenever she needed to talk. They'd become firm friends over the course of these past months, especially because neither of them had any other family close by to rely on. The bond they'd developed had gone beyond a work or a patient/midwife relationship.

'Noel did all the decorations at this time of year. He went all out until you could probably see our house from space with the number of lights he put up outside the house. It's not the same now. It's never going to be the same again.' Iona could see Katherine was trying hard not to get upset for the sake of the children, including the one who was due in the not-too-distant future.

'No, it's not, but that doesn't mean it can't still be good. You're a strong woman with two beautiful children and you'll get through this, I promise.' Iona's heart went out to the family. They had moved here from the city with the intention of providing a better environment in which to raise their kids, unaware their future would be cut short and leave Katherine to cope on her own with them.

Iona couldn't in good conscience turf Katherine back out to her husbandless home after a ten-minute check-up when she was this low. Her mental health was as important as the baby's welfare at this point; any distress could impact on the pregnancy.

'Listen, I have some time before my home visits. Why don't I go and make us a cuppa before we take all your measurements? I think we might even have a few choco-late biscuits stashed somewhere too.' An image of Fras-er's rectangular plastic tub with his biscuits counted to the last crumb came to mind. This was an emergency. He'd understand, and if he didn't, well, he'd just have to come and tell her so.

'Fraser's?'

'He's a medical professional. He knows chocolate cures all ills.'

Iona returned with a tray of sweet tea and biscuits for the two adults and glasses of milk for the children.

'Now, tell me how you're really feeling.' Iona made sure the kids were distracted enough not to eavesdrop on their conversation before she dug deeper.

That head start on her visits wasn't going to happen after all but it was more important for Katherine to be in a good frame of mind before she left here. Iona worked mostly on instinct and her gut was telling her she needed to be here.

'Stressed. Knackered.' Now she'd let the façade drop, the bags under Katherine's eyes were more noticeable and she was slumped against the pillows, crumpled under the weight of her woes.

'Let's start with the source of your stresses at the minute and we'll see if we can't tackle them one by one.' Tiredness wasn't unusual at this stage of pregnancy when the baby bump was so large it was impossible to get into a comfort-able position for a good night's sleep. However, depression could also be a factor and given recent events in Kather-ine's life it would be surprising if her mood hadn't been affected. The important thing was to recognise and ac-knowledge it so she could get help. Being a counsellor was one of the many unofficial roles a midwife was prepared to undertake to ensure a happy, healthy mother and baby.

'Apart from the obvious, there's all of the practical

things I'm left to deal with now Noel's gone. I mean, I was expecting him to pick up the slack with the shopping once I was at the whale stage. I can barely carry my own body weight, never mind lug bags of shopping around, even if I did have time, what with the school runs and the housework I've to do too. I can't keep on top of any of it and I've still to get the place ready for the baby coming.' Katherine let out a long, ragged sigh then helped herself to a biscuit and ate through the rest of her feelings.

'First things first, is there anyone who can give you a hand until the baby comes?' A good support system played a huge part in any pregnancy but here, with a grieving family heading into their first Christmas without their husband and father, they were going to need people around them more than ever.

'My parents are on a cruise over the holidays. They'll be back nearer my due date to help with the children but we're on our own until then. They weren't going to go but they've been so looking forward to it and I persuaded them we'd be fine. Unfortunately, Noel didn't have any family.' Katherine crammed another biscuit into her mouth.

'At least you'll have someone around when you're in hospital. Until then you know I'll help out wherever I can, and I'm sure everyone else in the village will want to offer a helping hand.' Everyone was fond of Katherine here and though she would never want to impose on people, Iona knew they'd fall over themselves to do what they could for her.

'Thanks, I appreciate that but I know we're not exactly local and everyone has their own family to focus on.' There was that note of resignation in Katherine's voice that everyone would be too caught up in their own lives and Christmas preparations to even think about driving out into the wilds to do a bit of vacuuming. She probably had a point.

Everyone except Iona had a life outside work and mightn't be as readily available as she was.

'You could put an ad in for a cleaner for a couple of weeks. I know it might seem like an extravagance but you don't want to be wearing yourself out. You should be taking it easy. It doesn't matter if your house isn't pristine in the grand scheme of things. You've done an amazing job of keeping your family going these past months so don't give yourself a hard time over a bit of dust. Order takeaways, let the kids decorate with cut-out snowflakes and finger paintings. Whatever it takes to get through the holidays. Remember Christmas is only one day and you've got a much more significant one coming up. Trust me, you'll all be more excited about welcoming a new baby into the house. Until then, stick a DVD on for these two and get a nap when and where you can.'

'That feels like such a copout.'

'No, it's called self-care. Your little ones are much more likely to remember you spending time with them than what decorations they did, or didn't, have this year. Speaking of which, did you hear Scrooge McColl enforced a ban on any festivities here so I have an overflow of garlands and sparkle? I'll come over and blitz your place with some magic fairy dust next time I'm passing if you want.'

'Ah, yes, I'd heard Fraser had put his foot down this year about the staff party too. I suppose he has a point. The drinking has had a tendency to get out of hand. It's better to keep these things separate so they don't muddy the waters at work.'

Iona couldn't help but being piqued at her friend for taking Fraser's side, no matter how on point her insight was, but she'd rather stay mad at him than think about that amazing lip-lock and the effect it had had on her last night. With his mouth on hers, his body pressed close, she'd been close to throwing away everything she'd worked towards, and walked away from, in a rush of hormones.

'Mu-um. I'm bored.' The first rumblings of discontent sounded from beyond the blue curtain as the children tired of their improvised art session.

'We'll be done in a wee minute or two. Get my phone out of my bag and you can play that game you like on it until I'm ready to go.' Katherine shouted instructions to her offspring and handed Iona her now-empty mug. 'See? I wouldn't get a minute to relax.'

It was probably true but at least those few minutes of normalcy over a cuppa with her friend had evened out the frown lines on her forehead. A chat seemed such a small thing but it could do wonders for mums, or anyone else feeling low or isolated. Once the baby came Katherine could socialise at the mother and baby club in the community centre but Iona would provide her company in the days leading up to the big event so she wasn't completely on her own.

If nothing else, this brief respite should have given Katherine some time to de-stress before she had her blood pressure checked, along with everything else. 'In that case, we'll get on with what you came in here for.'

'Sorry. I didn't mean to turn this appointment into a counselling session.' The small laugh was an improvement on the near-tears mood when Katherine had come in and proved Iona's theory that a listening ear could make all the difference.

'That's what I'm here for, to make sure you and bump are all right. You can call me anytime you need a friend. Now, do you have a sample for me?'

'Yes.' Katherine handed over the bottle with her urine sample for her to test.

'If you just pop on the scales, we'll make a wee note of your weight.' Increased weight was expected, indicating that baby was thriving, but as Iona plotted the digits on her chart they became cause for concern. Compared to the reading from the week before, Katherine had put on five pounds.

'I don't think I want to know.'

'You are growing another human being in there.' The dipstick she used to test the sample indicated the presence of protein and, combined with the excess weight, called for action.

Unbidden, Katherine lay back down on the bed and uncovered her belly so Iona could check the baby's size and position.

'Have you noticed any unusual swelling lately in your hands or around your ankles?' As Iona felt around the bump she could tell the baby remained in the head-down position and, compared to the last measurement, the growth seemed normal. If the baby appeared too big or too small she would need to order an ultrasound for a more accurate evaluation of its growth and check the levels of amniotic fluid.

'My ankles are puffier than they have been but that's not surprising with all the extra weight they're carrying.' With some help from her midwife Katherine took off her socks so Iona could see for herself.

The alarm bells were deafening now Iona could see the oedema causing the ankles to balloon and Iona was sure the skin around her patient's eyes were puffier than usual too.

'Any headaches, nausea or problems with your vision?' All the symptoms so far were pointing towards a diagnosis of pre-eclampsia that, if severe enough, could potentially cause serious, sometimes life-threatening problems and often warranted early delivery.

It was constriction of the blood vessels that caused the high blood pressure and this reduced blood flow could affect the liver, kidneys and brain. Such changes caused small blood vessels to leak fluid into the tissues, resulting in the swelling, and these leaks in the kidneys caused the protein from the bloodstream to spill into the urine. Although it was normal to have a small amount of protein in the urine, more than that signalled a problem. Less blood flowing to the uterus could lead to growth problems for the baby or placental abruption, where the placenta separated from the uterine wall before delivery. Early delivery was often needed to protect the mother's health and prevent a stillbirth.

'I suffer from migraines anyway and nausea comes with the territory. I just assumed it was the stress of the holidays. Why? Should I be worried?' If Katherine had had her nurse head on and not her busy mum one she would've recognised the signs for herself. Then again, all symptoms individually were common enough during pregnancy and it was only when they were added together they suddenly became something sinister.

'I'm going to check your blood pressure.' Choosing to avoid the question until they knew for sure there was a need to worry, Iona wrapped the cuff around Katherine's upper arm to take the reading.

With the tea and chat she'd had time to settle so elevated blood pressure now would solely be down to medical reasons and not outside influences.

A blood-pressure reading was considered high when the systolic upper number was greater than one-forty or the diastolic lower number was higher than ninety. Katherine's readings far exceeded acceptable figures. One high reading in isolation might not give an accurate picture, and results could fluctuate throughout the day but, combined with the other symptoms, Iona wasn't content to wait longer than necessary. The same reason she was willing to go with her gut instinct on the initial urine screening instead of waiting for the requisite twenty-four-hour sample collection.

'It's high, isn't it?' There was such resignation and understanding of the consequences in Katherine's question Iona didn't even have to answer it.

'Do you have any errands to run in town, or anywhere you could leave the kids for a while? I'd like you to come back this afternoon so we can do more readings. I think another urine test might be in order.' In place of twenty-four-hour monitoring there was another one-time test that could be carried out on a random sample. The protein-creatinine ratio could show signs of pre-eclampsia if it showed at least point three of a milligram per decilitre in results, creatinine being a waste product the kidneys should have filtered out.

'I was going to get a few groceries while I was here.'

Iona unfastened the cuff and noted the readings, which had cemented her suspicions. 'You go ahead and do that and I'll nip in and have a chat with Fraser about the next step.'

'If it's pre-eclampsia, we could both be in trouble, right?' Katherine lowered her voice as she stroked a hand over her bump, illustrating exactly where her fears lay.

'At the minute I'm simply being cautious. We need to do a few more checks but since you're not yet at thirty-seven weeks and your baby's developing well, it could be we just need to monitor your blood pressure closely for the rest of your pregnancy.'

If Katherine had been at the end of her term they would have had to think about inducing her but Iona didn't want the complications of an early delivery for any of them unless absolutely necessary. In certain situations a Caesarean section would be performed if there were signs mother or baby wouldn't be able to tolerate labour, but that would create more difficulties for Katherine when she had to cope back home alone with two other small children after the birth and the impossible task of resting.

'I'll see if I can find a babysitter for a few hours.' Katherine set her mind to practicalities and Iona was grateful for her calm acceptance as anything else could have exacerbated the condition.

'Good idea but don't over-exert yourself and I'll see you again in a couple of hours.' With the most reassuring smile she could give her, Iona helped Katherine down off the bed.

An official diagnosis was going to plunge the family into even more chaos over the festive period but this baby had to be delivered safely wherever, or however, that might happen.

'Right, kiddos. What do you say we go and get some comics and sweeties?' As most mothers were prone to do, Katherine hid her own worries so as not to upset her children and did her best to carry on as normal, so strong on the outside whilst inevitably crumbling on the inside. A widowed single mum with another baby on the way, facing a potentially life-threatening illness, couldn't help but draw compassion.

Before the family trooped from the room Iona threw her arms around her friend and hugged her close. 'We've got this, okay?'

She meant every word of the promise, even if that entailed having to consult Fraser on the case.

Fraser closed the door after his patient, even though there was no real need for continued privacy after he'd completed his paperwork and made his triage calls. On any other day he'd have been content to have an unimpeded view of clinic life but he wasn't ready to face Iona, or whatever new feelings he'd developed for her over the course of the past forty-eight hours.

Even when he'd been loading his old furniture into the

vehicle last night he'd known it was a mistake to return. That hadn't stopped him. Going against his own judgement was never a good idea and not an oft-practised one for this very reason—acting without considering all potential outcomes that could affect those around him was what drove everyone away from him in the end. Somehow he had to find a way to exercise some damage control with Iona for the sake of their working relationship. For his own peace of mind in future, one of their hot-tempered arguments would be preferable to the attraction that seemed to be drawing him closer and closer to her.

The knock on the door was a reminder he had more pressing matters to attend to than a romance that could never happen.

'Come in.' Fraser brought up the notes for his next patient on the computer screen to maintain a modicum of professionalism.

That pretence lasted merely seconds as Iona strode into the room full of purpose and Fraser's heart lurched at the first sighting of her this morning. With her uniform on and her hair tamed into relative submission, she was a different woman from the one who'd greeted him on the doorstep fresh out of the shower, but she had no less of an effect on him, his pulse leaping with the recollection of how she'd tasted on his lips.

'I...er...' Fraser had spent half the night and most of the morning in between consultations trying to construct a speech to excuse any behaviour that could have been misconstrued as inappropriate or an opening into a budding relationship. Only now, seeing Iona again, those words eluded him. He was fighting a losing battle when his better judgement was overruled at every turn by that primal need she'd unleashed within him.

'Katherine was here for her check-up and she's showing signs of pre-eclampsia. I know this is my jurisdiction but I wanted to consult with you on the matter since there could be certain complications for her family if she's admitted to the hospital.' If thoughts of their time together was on her mind, Iona didn't show concern for anything other than her patient. It was a serious enough condition that she was prepared to let him in on the case, not for his opinion but so they could work together on the best outcome for the family.

Fraser sat back in his chair and gestured for her to take the seat across from him to discuss their colleague's situation. 'How so?'

If she wasn't going to acknowledge what had transpired last night, he was more than happy to follow suit. He didn't need to give himself to another woman who had no qualms about rejecting him. It was a mercy in a way that it had happened before any notion of a romance had got off the ground, instead of waiting to deliver the blow when he'd invested everything he had emotionally in a relationship.

Iona cleared her throat, showing an uncertainty that he'd never seen her demonstrate before. She fidgeted with the hem of her skirt, unable to sit still, making her discomfort obvious.

A silver dagger engraved with guilt stabbed at his insides with the thought that stepping out of his regimented way of life and into hers had somehow caused her apparent distress. Although Iona would be the first to say not everything had to be about him.

'You know she lost her husband not that long ago and they have two other children?'

'Yes, we were all devastated for her.'

Fraser wasn't heartless and as the doctor who had treated Katherine's husband he was acutely aware of the loss she'd suffered. The death of a patient always stayed with him, in this case not only because the family was known to Fraser but because of the sense of powerlessness a terminal illness brought to everyone involved. Even doctors weren't immune to that frustration when all they could do was make the patient comfortable and pain-free where possible before the inevitable end. Any death felt like a failure on his part when his job was to treat illness and save lives, regardless that in such tragic circumstances no one had the power to stop fate in its tracks.

The conversation stalled with Iona waiting expectantly for him to say more on the subject than merely expressing sympathy. She didn't give him long to figure it out before she rolled her eyes and tutted at him.

'There's no one to mind the kids if she goes into hospital.' Iona spelled it out to him with a heavy dose of exasperation.

'Right. Of course. That's the last thing Katherine needs. She already has so much to deal with.' The family had had more than their fair share of bad luck and tragedy recently and it seemed it was going to continue for now.

'I've asked her to come back in a couple of hours for further blood-pressure and urine checks before I make the hospital referral. I thought that would give us some time to make a few phone calls to see what options are available so we can present her with the facts when she returns.'

'There are definitely no friends or family members she can call on since this is an emergency? I'd hate to think of the children being sent away to strangers when they are still grieving for their father.' Fraser wouldn't wish that on another young soul, having been through it at much the same age. Bereavement was such a confusing concept for children to deal with and they needed guidance and security—something that had been sadly lacking from his own father when he'd needed it most—to help them get through it. More upheaval and stress would have long-term consequences for the family unless someone was able to step in and find a way to smooth their path.

Unfortunately, Iona was shaking her head. 'Her parents are in the middle of the Caribbean somewhere on a cruise and not expected back before the New Year. Katherine might be able to hire a babysitter for an hour or two but there's no one close enough for her to ask to care for them long term. Two small children is a lot for anyone to take on in a village where nearly all the residents are over retirement age and those that aren't have young families of their own. With the exception of present company, of course.'

'So, that only leaves…'

'Temporary foster care.'

A solution they both knew would only upset Katherine more and terrify the children at the prospect of being sent away from the only person they loved to be at the mercy of strangers. That frightening journey into the unknown was something Fraser had been through himself when he'd been sent to boarding school away from everything he'd ever known. He'd much rather the children were able to stay with a familiar face, and together, if possible, to make the experience less traumatic.

It was difficult for a child to see the necessity of such actions, often blaming themselves for events as though they'd done something wrong and the decision to banish them from home was a form of punishment.

Although Katherine had no other options here, unlike his parents who'd simply decided they preferred not to have him around, Fraser doubted her little ones would understand it any better than he ever had.

'I hope it won't come to that and we might be able to sort things out for her. That's not something a member of our staff, a friend, should have to consider for her children. Have you broached the subject with her yet?' It wouldn't be the first time he'd had to contact social services regarding the welfare of children he suspected were being neglected, but it was a different story dealing with someone he knew personally was a fantastic mum going through a rough time.

'Not yet. I wanted to be clear in my own head about what would happen first before I overwhelmed her with information. Katherine isn't some addict or neglectful parent who doesn't deserve her children and I don't want her ever to be made to feel that way.'

'I'll do whatever I can to prevent that.' Not that either of them would sleep easily if her children were taken into care at all. 'Her parents really can't get home any sooner?'

Fraser didn't know what type of people they were but most parents, with the exception of his, would rather cut short a holiday to care for their daughter and prevent their grandchildren going into care.

'I'll try and convince her to contact them today. Perhaps I'll have more chance if she knows the alternative but even then, it's doubtful they'd make it back before she's admitted to hospital.'

Fraser could see why she'd brought the matter to his attention. Katherine was one of their own and they had to explore every available avenue before succumbing to the inevitable conclusion. He intended to do whatever he could to help.

'Have you spoken to the consultant at the hospital?' Fraser was already going through his list of contacts to see who he knew that could assist them in the matter.

'I'm going to phone now and get her booked in.' Yet Iona wasn't making any move to leave and start the ball moving.

Fraser lifted the phone on his desk and began punching in numbers. 'You do that. I have a friend who's a social worker. I'll ask her advice off the record about what can be done before we make anything official.'

It was a long shot but he was willing to try anything if

it would ease Iona, Katherine and the children's suffering in some small way during this difficult time.

Her soft, 'Thank you for understanding,' and slight up-turn of the mouth was sufficient payment.

How he wished someone like Iona had fought his corner for him to remain at home when his mother had become sick, and after her death, when his father had seemed to find his presence even more unbearable. If the McColls had had a family friend close enough to persuade them their son would be better off at home, his life might not have been ripped apart, never to be the same again.

CHAPTER FIVE

BY THE TIME Katherine arrived back at the clinic alone, Iona had already made arrangements for her to be admitted to hospital. The specialist Iona had spoken to was keen to monitor Katherine closely and try to get her blood pressure lowered.

'One pregnant lady reporting back with a full bladder as requested.' The humour wasn't quite covering up Katherine's fear and she was even paler than she'd been this morning.

'If you want to pop into the bathroom, we'll get another sample for testing.' In the meantime, Iona would call on Fraser for his input and find out if he'd heard anything from his social worker friend.

It was strange lapsing straight back into professional coolness towards each other after the heat they'd generated in her flat last night but it probably was best they didn't acknowledge anything had gone on and set aside their personal entanglement to focus on Katherine. Fraser had been very sympathetic to her predicament, most likely because of what he'd told her about his own childhood and losing a parent himself. Still, he didn't have to get personally involved and it said a lot about his character that he wanted to help get them out of this situation. His empathy with Katherine and the children was all the

KARIN BAINE   71

more remarkable given the cold relationship his parents had apparently fostered with him.

There'd been a couple of other things that had surprised Iona about their earlier meeting in his office. First, that he'd suggested making the call off the record, which was unusual as he wasn't known for going against procedure. In all likelihood it was his familiarity with the patient and the situation the family were in but there was a part of her wishing he'd done it for her sake too.

She'd also been rattled by the mention of his friend, a *she* by all accounts. A casual phone call to chat about the situation suggested he was acquainted with this woman on more than a professional level and that thought burrowed so far under Iona's skin to possess her soul that not even a priest with his Bible and crucifix could have driven it out. Obviously the upheaval of these past few days must've messed with her head if she was seriously thinking of herself as the spurned lover when she'd been the one doing the spurning. She had no right to have her claws out for his other potential suitors.

Iona's green-eyed imagination might have had something to do with the way she burst into his office. 'Katherine's back. Did you manage to speak to your *friend*?'

Fraser did a double take but didn't comment on her intrusion or her surly tone. 'I did get hold of Sandra, as a matter of fact.'

So he was on first-name terms with her.

'Iona?' An unusually timid Katherine appeared behind her and she cursed herself for not closing the door behind her.

Fraser rose from his chair and ushered them both in. 'Come in, Katherine, this concerns you too.'

He pulled another seat over so Iona could sit next to him and they could discuss this together.

She leaned forward so she was closer to her patient.

'As you know, there are some concerns about your current symptoms. The high blood pressure, protein in your urine and the nausea are all adding up to a possible diagnosis of pre-eclampsia.'

Katherine broke eye contact with him to focus on the hands clasped in her lap as she fought to hold it together. 'You still have the other test to do, though?'

'I've already spoken to the consultant at the hospital and they want you to come in. This afternoon.' There'd be more blood tests and if her uric acids were high, they might have to induce her.

The tears dripping down Katherine's face were a silent acceptance.

'They need to keep an eye on that blood pressure and treat it with whatever medication they deem necessary to bring it down to acceptable levels.'

'How long for?'

'As long as it takes. If things settle down they might permit us to monitor you at home but if they think you or the baby could be at risk there's a possibility they could keep you in until you're full term.'

This was out of Iona's hands now and solely down to the severity of the condition. She didn't want to scare Katherine any more than she wanted to give her false hope she could be home by dinnertime, but Katherine was in the profession so she knew the score and that they didn't have all the answers immediately to hand.

'What about the children?' As the implications of her impending hospital stay finally hit, Katherine fidgeted more and more in her chair, panic setting in. Iona should've taken her blood pressure before scaring her half to death.

'Where are they now?' It wasn't as though they were going to spirit her away without letting her say goodbye, as though she was going into witness protection.

'I managed to get Mrs McAdams to watch them for an

hour at the coffee shop but I couldn't possibly ask her to do that indefinitely. I can phone my parents but they'll have to arrange flights. What am I going to do, Iona?'

Iona had to swallow several times to prevent her airways closing as her friend implored her to help. 'There's a possibility they'll have to go into temporary care. Just until you're discharged or your parents get here.'

'No. No!' Katherine rose along with the pitch of her voice.

Tears were pinching the backs of Iona's eyes too as she attempted to calm her down. 'Social services will have to get involved once you're admitted. They have to make sure there's someone to take care of them.'

'I can do that. You said it yourself you can monitor my blood pressure at home. I can come here every day if I have to but nobody is taking my babies away from me.'

'We don't want to do that but you need to go the hospital for the sake of the baby. You'd never forgive yourself if something happened.' It wasn't a threat, it was a truth Katherine had to face. They weren't about to handcuff her and frogmarch her to the hospital but it was in her best interests to let them do comprehensive checks and begin the necessary treatment.

'I will never forgive myself if I have to put my children into care.' With her head now in her hands, she was sobbing so hard Iona was afraid she'd go into labour.

'It'll be okay, Katherine. Come on, sit down.' Fraser guided her back into her chair. 'I put in a call myself to a social worker friend of mine for some advice. Now, there's a chance we won't have to get them involved if you can come to an agreement with a family member to take care of the children.'

'It's not an option. I told you, there's no one until my parents get here. I need someone in the interim.'

'To be honest, Sandy confided in me that it's going to

be difficult to place them in emergency care so close to Christmas. If there's anyone you trust to mind them, I'm sure you could come to some arrangement with the local authority.' Reading between the lines, Iona could sense that it wasn't going to be easy keeping them together. Two young children who were still grieving for their father were a lot to take on when most people had already made their Christmas plans. Even those without family had an idea in their minds of how the festive period should pan out.

Katherine's children had done nothing wrong to find themselves in this situation and they deserved a better end to such an awful year. They needed to be spoiled and having so much fun they didn't have time to think about who was missing from their dinner table. Once their mother went into hospital they were going to be even more afraid and confused than they already were, and being split up and shipped off to strangers was going to make it harder to recover from for them.

All those horrible childhood experiences stayed with you long into adulthood, as Iona knew very well, and it was about time they had some positive memories of this year to cling to.

'I'll take them.' She didn't know who was more shocked by her outburst, Katherine, Fraser or herself. There'd been no thought to the practicalities of the suggestion, merely an emotional reaction to a situation she couldn't bear to witness without trying to do something about it.

'Are you serious?' The minute Katherine's face lit up with hope, her fate was sealed. There was no way she could back out now, even if the practicalities would have to be ironed out. She had no experience of raising small children but she could remember what it was like to lose a parent and it was that empathy that was making this decision for her.

'You need time to think this through.' Fraser was staring at her as though she'd gone mad, but why recommend a close friend should help if he didn't expect one to put themselves forward?

'Sometimes we just have to go with our gut feelings, and mine's telling me to do the right thing here.' Such was the common theme of their clashes, Fraser wanting to do everything by the book when she was happier to trust her instincts. Iona was usually justified in her actions and she hoped this time would not be the exception. Katherine literally had no one else and she certainly wasn't going to start analysing the pros and cons of her decision in front of her. This was one argument she wasn't prepared to give him.

'Can we really do this? I mean, the kids know Iona and it will only be for a few days…'

Damn Iona for giving Katherine this hope without proper consultation. Fraser didn't want the two mites to enter the care system any more than she did but he didn't want her to rush into something else without thinking, only to regret it. These were small children with real feelings who couldn't be picked up and set down on a whim. He was an adult and even he was having trouble keeping up with Iona's changeable moods.

Yet he couldn't deny he'd be happier to see the children go to Iona than imagine them spending Christmas without fun and love, the way he had too often.

He sighed and assumed the position of chief negotiator in the deal. 'There is the possibility of short-term foster care but you will have to notify children's services and request they assess you as a foster carer as soon as possible.'

'That shouldn't be a problem, surely? Iona is acquainted with the children and she's a medical professional. What more could they want?' In Katherine's mind at least, it would be the perfect solution to her current crisis.

Fraser wouldn't deny her peace of mind but it was going to involve more than signing a few pieces of paper. Thanks to Sandy, he was aware of some of the scrutiny Iona would be subjected to in order to assess her suitability as a carer. 'They don't know Iona as well as we do and they'll want background information for the social worker to submit a report for approval.'

'What sort of background information?' For the first time since riding to the rescue, Iona was frowning and perhaps thinking seriously about what was being asked of her. It sparked the embers of suspicion that there might be something she wasn't keen to share in her past. Maybe she wasn't as much of an open book as he'd assumed.

'Stage one will go into detail about your health, marital status, employment and accommodation.' They exchanged glances, fully aware her flat was barely adequate for a busy midwife without the addition of two small children.

'That could be a problem.' Despite her previous pride in her new home, even Iona could see the unsuitability of the premises for the purposes of raising children.

'They won't turn you down on the grounds that your flat's too small or you don't have a garden. I think it's more about ensuring the children have their own space.' It was going to be tight for sure, but Fraser could see Iona whipping the furniture back out if it would secure a place for Katherine's little ones to stay.

'Couldn't you just stay at our place?' It was natural Katherine would want to keep things as normal as possible but that didn't take into consideration the day-to-day practicalities of Iona's job.

'It's too far out for me to commute from every day. They're forecasting one of the worst storms of the year next week and neither I nor my expectant mothers can afford for me to get stranded up there. I don't think it would make practical sense unless you have a snow plough I can drive to work?' Not even the usually optimistic midwife could salve the crushing blow of disappointment falling on the plans of everyone in the room.

Crazy as this plan was, it was the only one available to save the children from going into care. It didn't matter to either of them where the children stayed as much as who they were with. They needed someone familiar enough that they felt safe and that could only be Iona, regardless of how unprofessional that was for a member of staff.

Fraser was acquainted with Katherine in much the same capacity as Iona. She'd been at the clinic longer than both of them, yet after these past couple of days he felt closer to Iona. Perhaps it was down to the time they'd spent together outside work, or because he'd already done her a favour he wouldn't have dreamed of doing for anyone else, but he was compelled to get involved. If only to make sure she wasn't taking on too much.

The kids deserved the best Christmas ever but her empty flat wasn't the right background to frame that happy scene.

As a child Fraser had seen both sides of the coin during the holidays. Either left at boarding school with those whose parents had lived abroad, going through the motions without any of the sentiment supposedly attached to the holidays, or at home, where his parents hadn't bothered about making a show for his benefit any more.

He'd always told himself that if he'd had a family of his own, they'd know they were loved, have all the joys most other children took for granted. After his disastrous attempt at a relationship this could be the closest he got to make that dream come true for some other frightened youngsters who didn't have a clue what was going on beyond missing the stability of a family home.

That big house, full of furniture and possible adventure, had always been missing the laughter of children and this could be one way to exorcise the loneliness there. It was vast enough to provide a solution and a home for the holidays. He could give Iona and Katherine a gift money couldn't buy.

He took a deep breath, contemplated getting a fellow doctor to prescribe him anxiety pills before he said what was on his mind. 'They could come to my place.'

The two women swivelled around to stare at him, mouths agape.

'Pardon?' It was Katherine who found the words to speak first. 'I could've sworn you just offered to take my kids in.'

'My house is closer to the clinic than Katherine's and bigger than yours, Iona, with a garden and rooms for each of the children. It makes more sense. On the understanding that Iona moves in too as their primary carer.' That covered all bases and though Fraser didn't have much experience of children outside the clinic, he was sure he'd do a better job than his parents had. Iona had made it clear in no uncertain terms that she didn't want to get involved with him on a personal level so that was the end of that issue. The focus would solely be on doing the right thing by this family and he wouldn't let any personal conflict impact on that.

'Iona?' Katherine turned to Iona for approval of this new radical plan.

The decision now rested with her and if she fought him on this it would be for more personal reasons than any excuse she could come up with.

'You'd have to go through an assessment too.' If she thought that would unnerve him, she didn't know him at all.

'Not a problem. I've got nothing to hide.' Even if they brought in a crack investigative team, all they would dig up on him was a list of disappointed exes who hadn't been fans of his regimented approach to relationships.

'You're really prepared to do this? To have me and two children move into your house indefinitely?' Iona was challenging him in front of Katherine to deliberately put him on the spot but he'd made up his mind.

'I don't say things I don't mean, Iona. Katherine needs someone for the children, you need a place for all of you to stay, and this way I can make sure you get to your shifts on time. It sounds logical to me.'

It wouldn't be beyond the realms of possibility for her to believe he was only doing this to ensure the running of the clinic wasn't affected by this madcap scheme. That was safer than letting her know he wanted to help her when he was doing that way too often to go unnoticed by anyone, including himself. He didn't understand what made Iona different from any other colleague that he put himself out to this extent, and he couldn't say he was happy about the disruption, but he'd become a slave to his conscience. Along with other parts of him he didn't wish to acknowledge.

'I'm sold. I'll be much happier having them in such capable hands. I can't thank you enough.' He'd managed to convince Katherine that his intentions were honourable, even if Iona continued to eye him with a certain scepticism.

'If we're all in agreement, perhaps I should put a call in to Sandy and see if we have to make this official?' He directed that at Iona, prompting her to give him a response confirming she was on board.

'I guess so. Katherine, you'll need to pack a bag for the hospital and get some of the kids' belongings together.' Hopefully as a sign of things to come, Iona was on her feet and setting the plan into motion. Since this was work-related-*ish* she would put more thought into this than she had over her last house move.

'Do I have time to take Hamish and Poppy somewhere first so I can break the news to them? I don't want to scare them by just disappearing in case they think the same thing's going to happen to me as their daddy.'

'We'll make time. The longer we take explaining to them what's happening, the better they'll understand it and make it easier for all concerned.'

As Katherine disappeared out of Fraser's office to get things organised, Iona hung back.

He supposed they weren't going to get far if he didn't deign to give away the keys to his kingdom again. He pulled out his desk drawer and retrieved his spare key, scribbled down his address on a scrap of paper and slid it across the desk towards her. 'If you put the postcode into your satnav, you should be able to find it.'

Iona closed the door and sat down again, clearly wanting a private conversation with him. Fraser braced himself to hear her regret over what had happened between them the previous evening and prepared to give her assurances it wouldn't happen again.

'Is there something else I can help you with?'

'It's about this background check for social services…'

There was a restlessness about her as she alternated between wringing her hands and rubbing her palms on her knees. He'd thought she'd seemed uneasy when he'd mentioned it but now he was worried that whatever she was about to tell him would jeopardise the whole plan, maybe even her position here if it was as serious as it appeared.

'Is there something bothering you, Iona?' Fraser couldn't begin to imagine what it was she was about to tell him but he knew it wouldn't leave the confines of these four walls if she trusted him enough to confide her secrets.

She stared at her hands, avoiding eye contact, her shoulders rising and falling with each shuddery breath, her usual confidence deserting her. 'I…er, I was in a difficult relationship a few years back. Married, in fact. The police were involved.' She took a deep breath. 'There are hospital records too.'

Fraser knew what she was trying to tell him, yet he didn't want to accept it.

'Iona,' he said softly, 'did he—did he hurt you?'

She lifted her head, the haunted look in her eyes breaking his heart. The idea that anyone could lift a hand to harm a curl on her head was as devastating as the thought of her cowering under the threat of violence. It took a special kind of coward to hit a woman and a worse one still who'd feel the need to crush her spirit. Someone obviously threatened by strong women who needed to exert some sort of power over her. Someone who'd never deserved to have her in their life.

'Andy exerted his control in physical form but he also inflicted mental torture on me too until I was a prisoner in my own home. It took a lot for me to leave him and retrain as a midwife so I could get my life back.'

In his position as a GP Fraser had witnessed a lot of domestic abuse cases, knew how quickly they could escalate into physical violence and how emotional abuse could cause as much damage. He'd referred countless patients to counselling as a result and treated many others for depression. For some the scars never healed but Iona was one of those rare survivors who'd used that trauma to become stronger and more powerful than the man who'd tried to dominate her through fear. It explained the mystery that had surrounded her move to the village as well as her habitual defiance against any form of control.

He was completely in awe of her strength. 'You're an amazing woman anyone would be proud to have in their life.'

With a swipe of her hand Iona erased any trace of the tears he'd seen forming. 'Anyway, I'm only telling you this because I'm worried it could affect my suitability as a guardian for Hamish and Poppy.'

There was no evidence of self-pity in her words when goodness knew she'd be entitled to it. It must've have been a serious domestic situation for police involvement and injuries to warrant hospital treatment. His urge to track down the person responsible for hurting her and give him a taste of his own medicine was almost as strong as his wish to hug her and comfort her when she was having to relive the nightmare. Neither of them would endear him to her. Instead, he did his best to allay her fears.

'I'm sure that will have no bearing on your current situation. You're not in contact with this individual any more, are you?'

Iona gave an emphatic 'No. We're divorced', letting him know she'd cut all ties with her abuser and giving him some peace of mind that there was no chance she'd let herself be dragged back into that nightmare again.

It was a very personal and painful matter she probably wouldn't even have shared with him but for her concerns over Katherine and her family. Fraser was thankful she'd been brave enough to walk away and start her life over again here in Culcranna.

'You've done nothing wrong and you have absolutely nothing to be ashamed about.' He wouldn't call her a victim when he knew she'd hate to be thought of in that way but that's exactly what she'd been. Now she was a survivor, a warrior who'd fought the battle for her life.

'Perhaps you could ask your friend if she thinks it could cause any problems down the line.'

'I can certainly do that if you want or we could ask Katherine about keeping this as a personal favour, without getting social services involved?' He knew fostering wouldn't be a problem, after all Iona wasn't at fault for an error in judgement. If that was the case every person who'd ever fallen in love with the wrong person would be barred from the process, himself included. Although this would go against proper procedure, he knew they'd all be happier with a more informal arrangement.

'Thanks, Fraser. I'll have a talk with her.' She didn't have to say any more than that as she left for him to understand how momentous this was for her, and him.

'No problem.' Fraser felt honoured Iona still trusted him enough to share the deeply personal information even after last night. Perhaps it was meant in some way to explain her reaction. She'd been hurt in the worst possible way and her fierce fight for independence had been her survival strategy up until now. It helped him understand her a little more and, just like that, he knew he'd been thrown back into the path of oncoming chaos.

CHAPTER SIX

'It's NOT TOO late to change your mind, Iona. I don't want you to feel obligated to do this because I have no one else.'

Iona and Katherine were sitting in the hospital car park, the children chattering away in the back seat at the prospect of their adventure in Fraser's grand house, with Katherine expressing her last-minute doubts about the arrangements.

'Definitely not. You heard Fraser. Between us we've got it all sorted.' Iona was still trying to get her head around his involvement in all this. Not only had he assured them they could manage this without outside interference, he'd managed not to treat her as a victim when she'd confided in him about her abusive past. He had been sympathetic without suffocating her, understanding that she didn't need a white knight to ride in and rescue her, offering help only when she'd asked for it. That alone was a big step for Iona after all this time of going it alone.

Fraser was full of surprises today. When he'd first suggested they stay at his house she'd nearly fainted. That wasn't in his senior partner's handbook and made him more human beneath that starched shirt.

'I thought I sensed some tension between you two and I wouldn't force you into a situation you're not comfortable with.'

Katherine was twisting the handle of her bag, which reminded Iona that the prospect of spending the next however many days in residence *chez* McColl was creating the same mass of knots in her stomach, but she couldn't let Katherine fret. Whatever was going on with Fraser, it certainly wasn't going to happen in front of the children. She'd shut down any notion of something happening between them and she'd never drag innocent minors into a potential messy relationship when she was proof of the damage that could do.

'Hey, neither of us would do this if we didn't want to. It's not in our DNA. Fraser's not that bad once he's off the clock. He helped me move into the flat and brought me some furniture to fit it out.' That was when the trouble had started and now she tended to forget he was a danger to her sworn singleton status.

'Maybe I really did read the signs wrong. Is there something else going on I don't know about?'

'No!' The denial came too fast and felt so wrong it was obviously a lie, but so much relied on this plan neither of them questioned it. 'Honestly, there's nothing to worry about.'

Although Iona veered between wanting to kiss or strangle Fraser at times. It was a blessing now that they hadn't fully given in to temptation when they were going to be shacked up together as stand-in parents for the foreseeable future.

She couldn't actually believe she was moving out of her home only a day after she'd moved in to live with another man. So much for the quiet Christmas she'd planned for herself but she could always do that next year, or the one after that. Katherine and the children certainly weren't having the jolly time they'd anticipated this time last year and they took precedence over Iona's self-indulgence.

'You will bring these two up to see me, won't you?'

Katherine reached around the back of her seat and fumbled to find the hands of her precious babes.

'Every day if I can.' It would be the only way to convince them that, unlike their father, their mum would recover and come home again.

Iona got out of the car to retrieve Katherine's things from the boot, allowing her some privacy to say her goodbyes. Understandably she was teary when she did eventually step out to join Iona.

'Take care of them,' she sobbed before swamping her friend in a hug.

'We will. Now, are you sure you don't want me to come in with you?'

Katherine shook her head and wiped her tears on the back of her hand. 'No. I'll be fine. Take them back to Fraser's and get them settled in. I'll call as soon as I can.'

'I promise I'll do everything I can to make sure they're happy.'

Things would work out fine if Fraser could straddle the line between senior partner and the guy she could rely on. If he swayed too far into the realm of either persona, their new arrangement could be in serious trouble.

'It won't be long now, guys,' Iona shouted into her rearview mirror to the bobbing heads of the children, who couldn't sit still. Thank goodness they were comfortable enough around her to see this as a holiday of sorts rather than something to fear.

It was Iona's nerves that were stretched tight enough to snap at any second in the unfamiliar surroundings. The night was creeping in and as they drove further and further into the wilderness there was a sense of being swallowed up by the darkness.

The lack of lighting out here wasn't helping. All it

needed now was for the car to break down and this would have all the markings of a horror movie.

Eventually they came to a set of gothic black wrought-iron gates, which opened on their approach. The security cameras mounted either side of the gates turned and followed her progression up the long, winding driveway. The security measures were good for the children's safety but not exactly a warm welcome to visitors.

Iona's jaw almost dropped into the footwell of the car as Fraser's fortress loomed into view.

'Is it haunted?' Hamish leaned forward between the two front seats to peer through the windscreen.

'Don't be daft. It's just a lovely big house with plenty of room for you and your sister to run around in.' The huge mansion sitting in the moonlight was the sort of place she imagined a gang of pesky kids and their Great Dane might come to solve mysteries but this was no cartoon, this was their real home until further notice.

The trio made their way to the front door and as it creaked open Iona half expected a tall, deathly pale butler, who'd probably been spying on them since their arrival at the gates, waiting to greet them. She was more surprised to find a hunky doctor in casual wear on the other side, imagining Fraser would have employed someone else to answer the door rather than have his usual routine disrupted by meeting his guests personally.

'You're here?'

She hadn't expected Fraser to be home, having thought he'd wait until they were in bed and less likely to disrupt his usual routine before he came back.

'I finished up earlier than expected and it occurred to me I didn't give you the security code for the gates.' There wasn't a hint that he'd come back for anything other than practical reasons. Yet the faded denim jeans and soft sage-green wool jumper he was sporting projected a friendlier image than his formal shirt and tie ensemble. He'd taken the time to change and since he wasn't expecting any other visitors she had to assume it was for their benefit.

'Can we come in?' The wind was beginning to howl around them on the doorstep and she pulled up the collar of her coat to act as a barrier against it.

'Yes. Sorry. The heat's on and dinner's in the oven. It's only chicken and chips, I'm afraid. I'm not much of a cook.'

'That makes two of us.' Iona followed the children, who'd run ahead, into the house, the idea of someone making dinner for her heavenly. He'd picked a child-pleaser too and although Fraser could deny it all he wanted, what mightn't be a complicated meal was something he'd gone out of his way to do for his house guests when undoubtedly he was more of a gourmet diner.

Hamish stopped dashing in and out of the rooms long enough to address Fraser. 'My mum says I'm the man of the house now and I have to take care of my wee sister.' He puffed out his chest in an attempt to appear bigger and braver than his young age portrayed.

'That's right but Iona and I are here to help out if that's all right with you?'

'Sure.'

Fraser played the big brother role perfectly, instead of barging in and taking over as he was prone to doing at work, so Hamish was suitably reassured Fraser wouldn't usurp his position.

'This is some place you have. I didn't know you ran a hotel business on the side.' They followed Fraser through the halls of his home, Iona as mesmerised by the elaborate décor as the two little ones.

'Very funny. I told you, it's my parents' place. I inherited it and I'm not entirely sure what I'm going to do with it yet.' When anyone else would've been jumping for joy over the riches bestowed upon them, Fraser didn't seem particularly happy about it. Up until yesterday she might have believed his resistance had something to do with being beholden to someone else's plans but he'd indicated there'd been some bad blood between him and his parents. On his part anyway. She couldn't imagine him inheriting the family fortune if they'd held a grudge.

'Complicated, you said. I can sort of see why. It's not everyone who has a couple of million spare to buy you out.'

'Not self-funded, I'm afraid. It's the family business.' He gestured towards the stern portraits lining the walls whose faces bore some resemblance to their casually dressed descendant leading the way to the kitchen.

Places were already set around the farmhouse-style table in the middle of the floor, which wasn't in keeping with the opulence on display elsewhere. The children were directed to their seats so Fraser could dish up dinner.

'This is cosy. I would've expected one of those mile-long dining tables in the Great Hall where you need a megaphone to be heard from one end to the other.' Iona poured drinks for everyone from the water jug on the table and watched Fraser's cheeks stain red at the joke.

'I prefer to sit in here.'

This old house had every cliché in the book and if she went exploring she'd be sure to find servants' quarters and maybe a housemaid or two hidden away. If he'd owned up about his status, he could have saved them a lot of trouble and provided a live-in nanny.

Whether from habit or a conscious decision to fit in, Iona noticed he didn't sit at the head of the table and pulled up the chair next to her. 'Tuck in, everyone.'

In an effort to set a good example to the other guests, Iona lifted her knife and fork and helped herself to the first hot meal of the day or, in her case, the week. She couldn't remember the last time she'd had a home-cooked meal and this didn't taste as though Fraser had tipped a couple of bags of frozen chips and chicken strips onto an oven tray. The giveaway was that it tasted of the food it was purported to be. He'd made them from scratch and added corn on the cob to their plates in an attempt to get the children to eat some sort of vegetables.

'This is lovely, thank you, Fraser.'

'Have you got loads of money?' Hamish, obviously taking a keen interest in the new surroundings, blurted out what anyone would've assumed on setting foot in the house.

'Hamish, it's not polite to ask that.' Iona scolded him, although it was human nature for that to cross a person's mind. There was no reason for Fraser to work at all as far as she could tell from the house and land he'd inherited. He was clearly dedicated to his profession since he could've retired at any point since his parents' passing. She was sure he could spend many happy hours alphabetising and arranging every expensive knick-knack here, instead of tending to the sick.

'It's all right,' Fraser said placatingly as the young lad leaned back on his chair, arms folded, potentially gearing up for his first showdown with authority.

'Hamish, please sit on your chair properly so you don't damage it.' If Iona had been aware this place was full of priceless antiques she wouldn't have taken responsibility for two small children and the damage they could do running amok here. It was surprising that Fraser had agreed to it at all. Along with being a babysitter, she was going to have to be a disciplinarian too. Neither she nor Fraser were parents to these children and there were going to be times the kids would no doubt push the boundaries so they had to set them early on.

'For the record, I'm not rich, but I do own the title of Laird and the land. As for the house, I'm trying to decide whether to break centuries of family ties and tradition and sell up. Anyway, if you're all finished, I'll show you up to your rooms.'

They traipsed up the grand staircase and along a carpeted hallway until Fraser stopped at a door on the landing. 'I thought Hamish would be comfortable in this room.'

The plush bedroom could've come straight out of a five-star hotel brochure but it wasn't very homely. Hamish set his superhero backpack on the bed. It was lost in the furnishings of a very adult room.

'It's very grown up, isn't it, Hamish?' Iona acknowledged Fraser's effort in preparing a space for Hamish and at the same time tried to convince the boy this was all one big adventure.

'There's plenty of space for you to put your things away and your bathroom is through there.' Their host gave a whirlwind tour, pulling out drawers and opening doors. An en suite bathroom was a luxury for Iona, who was used to house-sharing.

'You could put your pyjamas on, Hamish, and we'll come back when we get our own rooms sorted out.' They left the door slightly ajar so he wasn't completely abandoned.

'Poppy, you're next door to your brother.' The second room was less intimidating, smaller and decorated in neutral tones. Once they'd dotted Poppy's toys around and covered the bed with the favourite fluffy pink bunny blanket she'd insisted on bringing, it would be more child-friendly.

The door creaked behind them and a worried little face peered out at them.

'Come in, Hamish. Don't be shy. You're free to come and go as you please.' Fraser was usually so meticulous about everything being in its proper place it was strange to hear him being so welcoming to the boy. It was clear he wanted the children to be comfortable here, a magnanimous gesture on his part when Iona had the impression he never had been before.

'It's just a thought, Fraser, but could we bring another bed into this room? Perhaps Hamish and Poppy would prefer to stay together as he's promised to look after her for his mum.' She didn't want to embarrass the boy by suggesting he might be scared in that big room alone but wanted Hamish to think she was doing this to keep his sister safe.

'Sure. I'll show you to your room before I start shifting the furniture around,' Fraser said, striding out of the room at breakneck speed.

Iona took some pleasure in seeing Fraser disconcerted at the suggestion because it reminded her this congenial host act could be a façade and she shouldn't let her guard down just in case.

'This was my mother's room.' Fraser didn't give her the same warm introduction as the others into her new living quarters and she didn't dare enquire why his mother had had a separate room from his father.

'It's beautiful.' The scene before her was straight out of every little girl's fairy-tale. A four-poster bed and closet space big enough to fit her flat in, not to mention the roll-top bath in an alcove, was a fantasy come true. The floral wallpaper and thick pink carpet underfoot weren't to her taste but fitted perfectly in here.

'And where's your room?' She'd have to know in case of emergency, not because she was curious where he spent his nights.

'I'm down the hall.' In the other direction, she noted as he spun away from her.

'Thanks for this, Fraser. You didn't have to do this.'

'Neither did you.'

'No. We're a regular couple of heroes.' Iona laughed, not seriously fooling herself she was doing anything more than any other decent human would do.

'Or two people with nothing better to do over the holidays,' Fraser muttered, and left her to her own devices.

Iona heaved her bag onto the bed and unpacked the few things she had. There had been no way to predict how long they'd be here so they'd only brought the essentials for now. If anyone needed anything else, they could call home and get them. She eyed up the tub, wondering when she'd get an opportunity to use it. It wouldn't be tonight. She was exhausted and in danger of falling asleep and drowning in it and she had to get the children tucked up in bed at some point too. Although, judging by the thumping and banging coming from down the hall, they'd no intention of sleeping tonight. She had visions of them using the antique bed as a trampoline and Fraser presenting her with an extortionate bill for damages at the end of their stay.

'Hey, guys, can you keep the noise down in there?' Putting them into a room together might have been a bad move after all.

There was another loud thump against the wall, followed by the sound of muffled voices.

Iona sighed. She'd have to put her foot down tonight or they'd never get any sleep. She whipped the door open, fully prepared to read them the Riot Act if they carried on wrecking the place, except it was the Laird himself making all the racket and being reckless with the furniture. He had a bed base tipped on its side and was sliding it through the door, so focused he didn't appear to see Iona peeping at him. That's exactly what she was doing here, watching him as he stripped off his jumper—being a peeping Tom.

Fraser tossed his knitwear aside, revealing a tight white T-shirt layer. Iona scrunched up her face at being denied a sneaky glimpse of what lay beneath. Her stealth, however, was rewarded seconds later when he lifted the hem to mop the sweat from his brow.

Darts of lust targeted Iona's erogenous zones, the sight

of his taut stomach and that sexy V where his jeans rode low on his hips hitting bulls-eye after bulls-eye. When she realised the heavy lifting had ceased and she dragged her eyes back up his body to find she'd been caught ogling, she forced her buckling knees to carry her forward.

'You didn't have to do this on your own. I would've helped.' The belated offer of assistance should've been enough to deflect the fact she'd been gawping where she oughtn't, but the smirk on his face suggested otherwise.

'It's no problem. I can see you're busy.' He flipped the bed upright and manoeuvred it adjacent to Poppy's, mesmerising Iona with every flex of biceps she hadn't known he possessed under those buttoned-up shirts. Then he was on his hands and knees, tightening all the nuts and bolts and giving her a good view of his taut backside.

'I'll bring the mattress in.' She excused herself from the sight and the too-hot room to drag the mattress in from the hall.

Unfortunately her muscles weren't as well developed as Fraser's and she had to employ a combination of shoulder charges and kicking to move it.

'Let me try.' A large hand rested on her shoulder and almost collapsed her into a puddle. She hoped this hormonal mess incapable of functioning would return to her normal competent self soon once she got used to seeing a man around the house.

'Right, you two, into the bathroom to brush your teeth.' Leaving Fraser to the manly bed-building, she shut herself away to compose herself and remember who she was and who he was.

'Why's your face all red, Auntie 'Ona?' Poppy's scrutiny made her blush harder so she was forced to splash herself with cold water at the sink.

'It's hard work, moving furniture.' That was plain to

see from the trickle of sweat making Fraser's hair curl at the back of his neck.

Another splash of water and Iona kicked the door shut. She was too young to start getting hot flushes and needed her brain to compartmentalise this man back into his 'unsuitable dating material' box. The best way to stop daydreaming about his body was trying to wrangle two small kids into bed in a strange house but she knew once she did that the adults would be left alone and there were no guarantees her mind wouldn't start to wander again.

Fraser made up the spare bed and exited sharply back to his own room, collecting the jumper he'd cast aside along the way. Iona could put the kids to bed while he took some time to cool down.

He tugged his shirt over his head and tossed it into the laundry hamper in the bedroom with the rest of his clothes. At the last minute, before he stepped into the shower, he locked the bathroom door. He was going to have to remember he was no longer living alone.

His mind flitted back to Iona standing in the doorway, watching him so intently he may as well have been naked. The first blast of ice-cold water took away his breath along with the mixture of manual labour, anger and lust making him sweat.

While he lathered his body with soap, it was easier for him to fixate on never being able to please her than the memory of her predatory gaze sweeping over his body or he wouldn't leave this cubicle until he'd found some satisfaction.

He didn't want to be assigned a significant role in this scenario that he wasn't ready to accept. He was, however, considerate of the children's plight, and how they'd left the warmth and familiarity of home to be here. This wasn't a school full of stern masters and other frightened children but it could be equally as imposing. As an adult, and the owner, there were times it scared the hell out of him too.

Fraser had done everything he could to make them comfortable by cooking dinner and preparing their rooms, all the time wishing he'd retained some of the household staff after his father's death.

His best hadn't been good enough for Iona and though he'd shifted things around to suit he didn't think she'd find favour with anything he did. Ordinarily it didn't bother him if people took to him or not but he was sharing more of himself than ever with Iona and he wanted her to see the best in him. If he'd had any sense he would've volunteered for on-call duty this weekend and avoided crossing paths as much as possible then he wouldn't have to be constantly under her scrutiny.

Fraser slammed off the shower and towelled down before throwing on a clean shirt and jogging bottoms and padding barefoot downstairs to the kitchen. It was odd expecting to hear the chatter of other people when at any other time he imagined every creak and murmur might be the ghosts of his past come back to haunt him.

The house was quiet except for the sound of the kettle as he waited for it to boil and he assumed the others had all gone to bed after their fraught day. For the umpteenth time he wondered how he'd got himself into this mess. Iona. His life had been thrown into turmoil from the moment he'd held her in his arms and fried the logical side of his brain. How was he supposed to sleep now when the same woman was only down the hall from his bedroom?

'Oh. Sorry. I didn't realise you were down here. I fancied a cup of tea before bed.' Iona's unexpected arrival made him spill the hot water over the kitchen worktop and he had to move quickly before it scalded his feet too.

'Great minds...and all that.' Fraser grabbed some

kitchen towels and crouched down to mop up the mess he'd made on the floor.

Iona reached for another mug from the cupboard he'd left open.

'Sugar?' she asked, and it took him a few seconds not to respond with an equally sweet nickname to the one he'd imagined she'd bestowed on him.

'Not for me, thanks. It's in the container there beside the kettle if you want some.'

'I didn't mean to disturb you but you should know I'm a night owl.' Iona justified her appearance so late, even though this was to be her home too for a while.

'I'm more of a morning person myself but I suppose we should take the quiet times when we can get them, huh? Are they both down for the night?' Actually, Fraser didn't usually sleep long enough to have a preference, only catching a few hours in between when exhaustion finally overwhelmed whatever problems or memories had been keeping his brain awake. New people in the house were bound to bring him additional thinking time in the small hours.

'Out for the count.'

'We can take this into the lounge if you want. If we leave the door open, we can hear any little feet wandering around upstairs.' If they took their tea in there they'd have extra room to spread out and create much-needed distance between them.

'Are you sure you trust me not to spill anything on your antique rugs?' Iona was teasing but she didn't realise how close to the mark she was—Fraser was still afraid of causing damage to the family heirlooms. It had taken a long time to get used to being in charge around here and this was an act of defiance against the house rules for the sake of those he'd invited to treat his home as their own. It was just difficult for him to understand what that truly meant.

Not long ago he'd thought that was having a wife and children and now he didn't know if he'd ever have the right to the deeds without either.

'It's okay, I'll have the staff come in and clean up after you leave.' Fraser's deadpan delivery made her almost snort her tea back out.

'Do you actually have people who do that?'

'My parents did but I didn't see the need. Most of the time I only use the lounge and the kitchen, which I'm quite capable of cleaning myself, as you know.'

Iona's giggle, which came at his expense, nonetheless lifted his spirits. If they could find the funny side in his compulsions they were making progress.

Iona sat in the chair opposite him, her legs curled up under her. 'I know you have very valid reasons for not celebrating Christmas but you don't even have a tree.'

Which, apparently, was the crime of the century. It suggested his life was in some way lacking because he hadn't bothered chopping a tree down to stick in a bucket in his front room.

'Last year wasn't a great Christmas for me either. My… er…girlfriend left me. Just after I proposed to her. I wasn't in a hurry to be reminded of it.' It hadn't crossed Fraser's mind to decorate because he was supposed to be the only soul in residence. When he'd had a partner, a vision of a future together and there'd been something to celebrate, he'd done the whole festive frivolity along with everyone else, but, as in his childhood, it had turned out to be fake and a waste of time pretending Christmas was something special.

Talking about it now wasn't as painful as it once had been. It was a positive sign that he was beginning to move forward and not letting either event define who he was. That should probably include no longer allowing bad memories to taint future holidays.

'I'm so sorry. I don't want to make you uncomfortable in your own home but the children could be here for Christmas. It's only a few days away and I'd like to try and make it special for them. Would you mind if I decorate? I could limit it to their room if you'd prefer and you wouldn't have to do anything except say yes. They're still little enough to believe in the magic and I don't want to spoil it for them. Your house is beautiful but it's not very child-friendly.'

Didn't he know it. When he hadn't been at school, abiding by the rules there, he'd been restricted by the list of dos and don'ts at home. Don't make too much noise. Don't leave toys where people could trip on them, dress smartly, don't talk back... He'd never been free to explore childhood without a scolding. There hadn't been much reason to change anything in the house once he'd found out a family was off the table for him.

'This has never been a fun environment for raising children.' He'd been more of an intruder when he'd been home, having to be careful not to disturb his mother, who had invariably been in bed, exhausted at the very thought of having him here. These walls echoed with the loneliness of his childhood and he'd have changed everything in a second if Caroline had accepted his proposal and set up home with him. After she'd left there hadn't seemed any point in changing anything.

'My mum used to put on the whole show with the tree, the presents and the big family dinner. It was wonderful. Except for the ever-present threat of my dad's temper, which would explode when he found fault with the smallest thing. Then that lovely tree, the thoughtful gifts and the dishes of food would end up smashed on the floor.' Iona clutched her tea close to her chest and looked smaller than ever.

Their constant battle over power seemed to be about

asserting their right to be heard when they'd both been nothing but casualties of their past.

'I guess a domineering father is as damaging as a disinterested one,' Fraser mused aloud, although Iona's experiences of ruined celebrations had taken her in the opposite direction from his attitude.

'So you can see how important it is we get this right?' Iona didn't have to guilt-trip him. Fraser had accepted that responsibility when he'd agreed to host them here. That's why he was so afraid of getting it wrong. He trusted Iona had enough experience of at least one loving parent that she had more clue than he did about how to do this.

'You have free rein. Go tinsel crazy around the house with my blessing.' He was sure he could stomach it for a few days.

'Are you serious?' As soon as he said it her eyes lit up like fairy lights and she dropped the defensive body language.

Fraser winced as she set her cup on the floor, flattening a circular patch of the deep-pile carpet, but let it pass since she looked so happy. He didn't want to be another man to make Iona miserable. Her enthusiasm was contagious, his smile growing to match hers. What harm could there be in letting her loose with a few ornaments? The house wasn't governed by the health and safety rules of the workplace or even those set by his parents. As he had to keep reminding himself, he was free to do as he pleased and now so was Iona.

'I'm serious. Honestly, I'm not the monster you think I am.'

She bounced out of her seat and launched herself at him. 'Thank you. Thank you. Thank you.'

She landed a smacker of a kiss on his cheek before she whispered, 'I've never thought of you as a monster.'

In that second all his icy edges melted and he would've

let her redecorate the whole house if she'd asked. There was something about her and her quest to fix everyone that made him think she might be able to fix him too.

'Let's try and keep it that way,' he eventually managed to get out after the shock of her touch and his need to please her ebbed away.

He ignore the urge to nuzzle into the cloud of soft curls falling around his face and waited until she backed off before he could breathe again.

'I'll make a list of everything we have to do. I've never planned a family Christmas before.'

'Neither have I.' Fraser had never even considered he'd truly been part of one and now there was a possibility he'd always be of the opinion it should include Iona and a kid or two.

CHAPTER SEVEN

'I HAVE TO make a few patient calls then I'll pick the kids up from their after-school club.' Iona checked in with Fraser after ensuring he didn't have any patients in with him.

'Should I expect a lorry load of fake snow and a herd of reindeer to meet me on the drive when I get home?' He spun around in his chair, arms folded across his chest and giving her that bright smile that was fast becoming a familiar fixture. They'd come such a long way since the day they'd fought over the decorations here at the clinic and she was glad of it. Now she was comfortable enough to walk into his room and plant her backside on his desk.

'Unfortunately, it was too short notice to get the reindeer. They're fully booked until the New Year. You might get the snow, though—I hear they're predicting a white Christmas this year.'

'I'm sure the kids will love that. Not so good for the rest of us who still have to work. Speaking of which, I've managed to get cover in for Christmas week in case we're still playing happy families.'

That's exactly how it had seemed this morning as she and Fraser had teamed up to get the children ready for school. She'd made sure they were washed and dressed before they all sat down to a Fraser breakfast special of freshly made French toast and bacon. He'd also packed lunches for everyone as they headed out on the school run. There was definitely something to be said for being organised when they were all benefitting from it and starting the day calmly instead of the chaotic mess it could've been, left to her.

'Oh, good. I'm not planning on going anywhere but babies have a habit of not sticking to the schedule. With you at home that means we've got things covered.' She high-fived Fraser.

Home. How quickly she'd come to think of that huge house and the inhabitants as somewhere she'd every right to be and wanted to be. Not every housemate was someone to dread, just as living alone didn't have to be everything. Last night, chatting with Fraser, had reminded her there wasn't always something to fear from sharing her personal space. It could actually provide a sense of well-being to have someone to unwind with and talk to. Until now Iona hadn't realised the extent to which she'd isolated herself. Outside work and patients she didn't have anyone to call on for a chat or a shoulder to cry on if she needed one, and there was something reassuring, therapeutic even, in having company other than her own.

For too long she'd associated any form of relationship as a hassle, something to be endured or avoided at all costs. Simply having someone who understood her, who was willing to compromise his needs to accommodate hers, showed her there was something different out there if she wanted it.

'Should I bring something home for dinner?' He'd swivelled around again and tossed that word casually over his shoulder, which made her shiver every time she thought of him waiting there for her.

'That would be great. I've promised Hamish and Poppy we'd make it to the hospital for visiting later then we can start decorating. I'll get some Christmas supplies with them after school.' They'd have more than enough to keep them busy until bedtime and hopefully seeing their mum would help settle them. According to the staff member she'd spoken to this morning, Katherine's blood pressure remained high and they weren't prepared to send her home yet.

Fraser stopped typing momentarily to glance at her. 'Is there anything else I can do for you?'

Iona was aware her continued presence, sitting here, was disturbing his otherwise perfectly arranged desk but she was enjoying this new easy atmosphere between them too much to leave.

'Um, no, I don't think so.'

'You're sitting on my notepad.'

She shifted her position slightly so he could retrieve his precious notepad but hadn't anticipated the effect his hand brushing against the curve of her backside would have on her. The joke had well and truly backfired and her attempt to provoke him had succeeded in raising her own temperature.

She leapt off the desk as though someone had started a fire beneath her, things suddenly feeling too hot for her to handle.

'I'll see you at home,' Fraser called after her, and now she really couldn't wait to finish her shift.

Iona phoned around her patients to give test results and check in with her ladies before she clocked off for the day. Once she'd finished her shift, any emergencies would be down to the duty midwife. The midwives from neighbouring clinics took turns at covering nights and although it was a large catchment area they weren't overly stretched with callouts.

She was already putting her coat on as she dialled

Angie, one of her first-time mums, so she could get started on her evening plans as soon as possible.

'Hi, Angie, it's Iona here. I'm just calling to tell you your last test results were all clear. The antibiotics seemed to have cleared up your UTI so there's nothing to worry about.' She turned off the light and grabbed her car keys from the desk.

'Thanks, Iona, that's a weight off my mind. It's been one urine infection after another lately.' The heavy sigh was a standard response from most of her patients in the later stages of their pregnancies as they struggled to even tie their own shoelaces. Although she'd never been pregnant, Iona could understand the frustration of not having a say in what happened to you. Andy had taken that right away from her with the physical and emotional torture he'd put her through until she had been too frightened to make any decisions for herself in case he disagreed. Thankfully, those days were long behind her and she was a different person now from who she had been then.

'How are you feeling otherwise?' It had only been a couple of days since Iona had seen Angie at the clinic but it was a question it was always necessary to ask in case anything untoward crept in between appointments.

'Some heartburn at night and I don't know if this is anything but my hands and feet have been really itchy. It could be an allergic reaction, I suppose, but I haven't changed my washing powder or anything recently. It's probably nothing.' While Angie was talking herself out of the significance of any symptoms, the comment managed to stall Iona's exit.

'What about the baby? Is he still moving about plenty?' Adrenaline was rushing through her system at the prospect of what this could mean for her patient but she didn't want to scare her.

'Not as much today but I was up late last night because

I couldn't get comfortable at all.' There was a yawn to illustrate the lack of sleep.

'The itching was more noticeable at night?' Iona retraced her steps back into the office, turned the light on and retrieved Angie's file.

Mild itching itself wasn't uncommon during pregnancy as the skin stretched to accommodate a growing belly but it could be symptomatic of a more serious condition.

ICP, intrahepatic cholestasis of pregnancy, was a potentially serious liver disorder, often characterised by itching when bile acids, which should have flowed from the liver to the gut to aid digestion, built up elsewhere instead.

To get a conclusive diagnosis they would need a variety of blood tests to check liver function and measure bile acid levels but time would be of the essence, especially if the baby's movements had reportedly slowed. There was a high risk of stillbirth for those with an elevated BAL. There was no cure and with Angie in her thirty-seventh week of pregnancy it was possible the hospital would want to induce labour to prevent the worst from happening.

'Angie, is Chris there with you?' This would go much easier if she had her husband there to support her.

'No, he's at work. Why?' That element of fear Iona hated hearing in her patients' voices when she had to deliver distressing news was there, turning her own blood to ice.

'I don't want you to panic but I would prefer it if you went to the hospital to get checked out and make sure everything's all right.'

'Why? What's wrong? Chris won't be home for hours— he's working in Aberdeen. Is my baby in trouble?' The panic gradually picked up pace and there was only one thing Iona could do.

'Everything's going to be fine. I'm being cautious but

I'd prefer to get you to hospital for a scan to make sure the baby's not in any distress. I'll drive you myself.'

'Should I have my overnight bag ready?' Angie sniffed back the tears but she already sounded calmer that she wouldn't go through this alone.

'That mightn't be a bad idea.' Not only would it give her something to distract her until Iona got there, the obstetrician might decide to keep her in.

'I'll phone Chris and let him know.'

'I'll be with you as soon as I can and, Angie, please don't worry.' Words were never enough to soothe a scared mother-to-be but the presence of an experienced midwife often put her mind at rest that someone knew what they were doing in the circumstances.

Iona was in the car and on her way before she'd hung up. Technically the call should have gone to the duty midwife, who probably would've told her to phone for a taxi or rung straight through for an ambulance, but Iona thought there was more chance of keeping her calm by doing it herself. She would do the handover, of course, leaving Angie in the care of the consultant lead team at the maternity unit, but having a familiar face for most of the journey could make all the difference to a woman's first experience of pregnancy in such difficult circumstances. On speakerphone, she managed to call ahead and let the hospital know she was bringing Angie in.

This kind of crisis was the reason Iona could never be a normal wife and mother with responsibilities. It would only take her back to those dark days of having to account for her every move outside the house until it was easier to simply stay put.

Wait. This week that's exactly what she was supposed to be and she'd failed at the first hurdle. Not only was she going to be late for the school run but she was going to have to renege on the promises she'd made to her surrogate children.

The steering wheel took the brunt of her temper as she lashed out and swore. It was going to be harder to juggle motherhood and work than she'd imagined, as she'd become so accustomed to doing what she wanted when she wanted. Iona wasn't used to thinking about other people outside work or relying on anyone but herself.

Now she was going to have to depend on Fraser, her pseudo-husband, to jump in and save the day. It was going to take hours to get to the hospital and back, by which time she'd have missed visiting time, dinner and Christmas decorating. She wasn't looking forward to disappointing the children or putting in an SOS call to Fraser. Already she could see there was a fine line between controlling and being in control when it came to family obligations, and she was a long way from both. Fraser might have the better temperament for taking care of children after all. Gut instinct was all well and good but she had others to think about now and a flaky parent was as damaging to the bonding process as an overbearing influence. She prayed he'd step up to cover her inadequacies until she could make it up to everyone later. If she made it back at all before bedtime.

'You're rubbish at this.' Hamish provided the harsh critique as Fraser lifted the tray of charcoal that purported to be the walls of their gingerbread house.

'I'm doing my best.' He dumped the charred remnants on the draining board along with the other gingerbread rubble from their last attempt. They'd managed to stick three walls, and Fraser's fingers, together with the icing before it had collapsed on itself.

'It's yummy.' Poppy helped herself to a broken piece of the front door and wandered off again. It was nice to know it hadn't been a complete waste of time.

'My mum makes good gingerbread. I wish she was here.' Hamish kicked the leg of the kitchen table with the toe of his scuffed shoe, which ordinarily Fraser wouldn't have stood for but he understood that feeling of being let down by Iona tonight.

How many times had he stood waiting at the school entrance, bag packed and ready to go home, only to be told at the last minute no one was coming for him after all? Enough to stop him trusting a word his parents had said. Young children didn't understand the reasons you flaked out on them, they didn't care about anything except the fact you didn't stick to your word. Once that trust was lost it was difficult to get back. These two had every right to be annoyed. It wasn't as if Iona couldn't have arranged for someone else to provide a taxi service, no, she'd chosen who'd deserved her attention and it certainly hadn't been the master gingerbread builders here. Still, it wasn't going to help lift the mood if he let rip at Iona when she did come home. Parenthood was new to both of them and they were learning on the job.

Fraser pulled over a chair and sat down so he was at eye level with the disgruntled seven-year-old. 'Listen, this isn't easy for us and I wish it was your mum here baking for you, and she will be, soon. I know you're disappointed you didn't get to see her but I'll do my very best to get you there tomorrow.'

'Sure...' Hamish didn't look up from his feet, already cynical about trusting the word of an adult.

It took Fraser to physically tilt his chin up to make him look at him. 'Hey, I mean it.'

Hamish didn't seem convinced but he did stop taking out his anger on the furniture and ran off to find his sister.

Tonight had been tough, thanks to the last-minute change of arrangements. By the time Fraser had finished at work and picked up their new dependants it had been too late to make it in time for visiting at hospital. Hamish had been in a foul temper since and Poppy much too quiet for a five-year-old.

Fast food hadn't managed to lift their spirits and neither had the impromptu art class he'd set up. The lack of decorations they'd been assured would be up today hadn't gone unnoticed by the children so he'd persuaded them to make their own. Although their paintings were colourful, they weren't enough to brighten up the huge room.

He'd let them stay up well after their bedtime in the vain hope Iona would show up before they retired for the night. The kitchen massacre could be dealt with after that.

'I think it's time you put on your pyjamas and brushed your teeth.'

'Iona said—' It was Poppy's turn to protest.

'I know, Iona promised we'd decorate but she got caught up at work.' In her brief call she'd told Fraser she was driving her patient to the hospital but, knowing her, she'd stayed on for moral support too. A quality he'd admire in her if it wasn't for the two disappointed faces staring at him.

It was better for him to imagine she was hand-holding a frightened pregnant woman than that she'd been in an accident on that dark, potholed road back to civilisation. Like it or not, they were a makeshift family as a result of their recent decisions and apparently that entailed worrying about all members, every minute of the day. It wasn't a responsibility anyone should take lightly and, in hindsight, it had probably been fortunate Caroline had changed her mind about the prospect of family life before they'd married or he could've been left as a single father.

As Fraser began seriously contemplating reporting Iona as a missing person, car headlights slowly made their way up the drive. Although relieved she was safe, he was going to have to confront her about the childcare situation.

Hamish and Poppy ignored his request, watching Iona through the window with him. When she turned the key in the front door there was a posse waiting for her.

'Hello. Sorry I'm late, everyone. I had to take a very poorly patient to hospital and I didn't want to leave her on her own.'

'Hi. How is she?' Fraser rammed his hands in his pockets after he noticed they were covered in icing and glitter.

'They're keeping her in to do a trace but her husband is with her now.' Iona flung herself into a chair and kicked off her shoes.

'I hope everything works out all right.'

'Me too.'

'There's some dinner left in the oven if you're hungry.' He'd saved some leftovers as he'd never seen her take a proper meal break in all the time she'd been at the clinic.

'Starving. Thanks. How did you get on today?'

'We did some painting and tried our hand at building gingerbread houses. It didn't go very well.' An understatement she'd see for herself next time she stepped into the kitchen but it was important she knew he'd done his best to keep the children entertained in her absence. Despite the fact that they were still upset, he'd genuinely wanted to get involved with them and had shaken off any notion he'd be as bad a parent as his own. Far from putting the idea of fatherhood far from mind, he was afraid it was strengthening the case for having children of his own. Unless he found a partner who was completely committed to the idea with him, it was a non-starter anyway.

'Sounds fun. Sorry I missed it.'

'Did you get Christmas stuff?' Poppy piped up with the question that had prevented her from going to bed, afraid of missing something.

'I didn't get to the shops in time, sweetheart. I stopped off at the petrol station but this was all I could get for now.

We'll get more tomorrow.' She handed a bag to Poppy, who proceeded to sit cross-legged in the middle of the floor and empty out the contents.

One by one she held up the items—strands of silver and gold tinsel, a packet of foil-covered chocolate tree decorations, plastic mistletoe and a tree-shaped car air freshener.

'You said we'd have a proper tree.'

Iona attempted to hug the little girl but was brutally shrugged off. 'We'll get one tomorrow after school.'

'Unless you have something better to do.' Hamish gathered up the unwanted gifts, stuffed them back in the bag and dumped it at Iona's feet. Fraser was beginning to feel sorry for her. She hadn't intentionally hurt them, had simply tried to do the right thing by everyone. The last thing she would've wanted after a long day, and evening, was to face more stress at home.

'You heard Iona, we'll do everything tomorrow. It's late and we're all tired.' He gave his child-minding partner a hand up so they were both imposing their authority together from a higher vantage point.

'We couldn't see Mum tonight because of you,' Hamish spat, and caused Iona to flinch.

'Enough, Hamish. Tomorrow, you were told. Now, go up to your rooms and get ready for bed.' It went against all his instincts to scold the children but he couldn't let them attack Iona. It would undermine their position as the adults in charge if they didn't set boundaries from the start.

Unfortunately, it also put him into the doghouse alongside Iona as far as the sullen child was concerned.

'You're not my dad and you're not my mum. I hate you both.' Hamish stomped out of the living room and up the stairs. Fraser's heart ached for him as he was clearly missing his two parents.

Iona stared open-mouthed as Poppy trotted after him

and the sound of the bedroom door slamming echoed through the house. 'Now what?'

'Let him cool off for a while then I'll go and have a talk with him.' Fraser had never wanted to get emotionally involved but since he had some understanding of what the boy was going through he might be in a better position to talk him round.

A dazed Iona sagged back down into the chair.'

'I really didn't mean for them to feel like an afterthought but Angie had suspected ICP and this is her first baby. I'm an idiot for thinking I could get away with postponing their evening and making up for it with a bag of tat from the garage.'

'Don't be so hard on yourself. We're dealing with two vulnerable young children. They're scared and have had such upheaval they need to lash out at someone and, unfortunately, that's you tonight.' Fraser put an arm around her shoulder and gave her a squeeze to let her know he was on her side.

'You heard Hamish, he hates me, and I'm pretty sure Poppy's right there with him. Even if he hadn't said it I could feel the animosity in the atmosphere as soon as I stepped into the room.' Years of walking on eggshells had finely tuned that skill, anticipating shouldering the blame for whatever perceived misdemeanour she'd committed to justify Andy's foul mood. Although, in these circumstances, the anger directed at her was understandable.

'Now, now, don't go getting all sorry for yourself. I do believe he said he hated us both. Something I'm choosing not to take seriously or personally when he's clearly upset.'

Iona appreciated Fraser's attempt to make her feel better but so far it wasn't working. 'Nice try, but we both know this is my fault. I just hope you won't hold it against me. I'm trying, I really am, but it's difficult for me too. I'm not used to factoring anyone else into these last-minute decisions, or trusting anyone other than myself. That's why I felt the need to take Angie to hospital myself and why I'm struggling to work as part of a team here with you. It's going to take time, Fraser, for all of us. I've relied only on myself for so long none of this is coming naturally to me.'

She was bone weary, leaning into him and making him wish they could put the whole saga behind them and relax until tomorrow, when they had to do it all over again.

'For me neither. They'll forget all about it once they get to see their mum and they have a lovely sparkly Christmas tree to stare at.'

'I hope you're right.'

'Always,' Fraser said with a grin. 'Look, I can identify with the kids but that doesn't mean you should be punished for doing what you thought was the right thing. My parents sent me to boarding school at an early age and let me down time and time again, telling me they were coming to pick me up, getting me excited, only to change their minds at the last minute. At that age you're left feeling as though no one cares, that your feelings don't matter, even when there's a perfectly reasonable excuse.'

'Gee, thanks for making me feel better.' Now she had the added guilt of making Fraser relive his abandonment issues too.

'I'm simply trying to explain the fear hidden behind the surface anger. As long as you follow up on your word tomorrow, I'm sure they'll forgive you.' Fraser's wounds obviously still ran deep from his experiences but that was probably why he'd bonded with the children so quickly.

Iona was afraid her actions would somehow exclude her from the circle of trust they'd been working on together.

'What about you, Fraser? Will you forgive me?' She'd hurt him on several occasions and eventually she'd run out of lives with someone who'd obviously been so let down in the past.

'I did, the moment you came home safe.' Fraser tilted her chin up so she was looking into his eyes, and seeing the truth of his words reflected there made her heart melt. The knowledge that he cared enough about her to worry made her want to wrap herself up in his arms and the warmth of that beautiful sentiment.

He dropped his hand away so quickly she thought she'd imagined the whole exchange. 'Now, come on and we'll get you some dinner.'

It was obvious he wanted to keep things light between them so she simply had to file away the moment along with all the other ones they couldn't talk about. 'I wouldn't say no. I didn't dare stop for any on the way home. The wind is picking up out there and I had visions of my wee car being blown into a ditch or a tree falling on my roof.'

'In that case, we should get your dinner on in case there's a power cut. You start reheating and I'll hunt for candles and torches.' They made their way to the kitchen, where Iona picked at the gingerbread ruins lying around as she waited for the microwave to ping.

From now on they had to work as a team. It was the only way they'd survive.

The reheated pizza and fries were no substitute for Fraser's home cooking the previous night but Iona's rumbling belly was past point of caring.

She'd expected disappointment and guilt about not following through on her plans with the children but the full blast of Hamish's rage had almost finished her off. Judging by the bomb-hit worktops she wasn't the only one who'd had a tough day.

'Thanks for covering for me,' Iona said after swallowing a mouthful of the wine Fraser had poured for her. He hadn't had much say in the matter but he hadn't tag-teamed the others to point out the extent of her failure so she was grateful.

'What did you think I'd do? Leave them somewhere with a sign around their necks saying, "Please take care of me"?' Fraser was trying to make her laugh and he succeeded.

She'd been expected an 'I told you so' once she realised what a great undertaking this whole thing had been. If they'd been in this position a month ago she'd have been horrified at the thought of leaving Fraser in charge of the children. It wouldn't have been a stretch to imagine him marching them around the house in regimented fashion, issuing commands. Since getting to know him properly, she'd almost become too complacent that he was up to the job.

The paint-splattered surfaces and baking attempts showed how hard he'd tried to cover for her without expecting, or receiving, a gold star for his efforts. Thank goodness he was in this with her because it was clear now she'd never have managed them, and work, on her own.

'Maybe you should do that to me.'

'Something tells me you wouldn't be willing to let anyone take care of you.' Fraser's insight was spot on but she was willing to let him clear away her dirty dishes for her.

'Take care of me, yes. Take charge of me, definitely not.' It was a warning shot that he shouldn't dare to try but as she locked eyes with him he didn't look away. As if he was telling her he was up to whatever challenge she set him.

CHAPTER EIGHT

An almighty crash interrupted Iona's late supper, so loud it made her jump out of her seat. 'What the hell was that?'

She'd seen plenty of horror films to know big houses were playgrounds for ghosts, ghouls and everything else that went bump in the night.

'That was the front door being slammed.' Fraser bolted in the direction the noise had come from but his explanation didn't put her any more at ease. The solid wooden door didn't open and close by itself. Either someone had come in, or gone out, and both scenarios sent chills through her cold enough to freeze her bones.

'I'll go and check on Hamish and Poppy.' She left Fraser walking out into the night and took the stairs two at a time in her haste to make sure they were safe.

On opening the door, she was relieved to see Poppy was fast asleep. Hamish's bed, however, was empty and his backpack missing along with the few personal possessions he'd brought with him.

All the blood seemed to drain away from her body until she was sure her empty Iona shell might collapse at any second. It was only the fear of Hamish being outside alone in the dark keeping her upright and propelling her downstairs.

She ran out onto the porch to locate Fraser, not taking

time to find her shoes when it was her fault the child was out there somewhere exposed to the elements. 'Hamish is gone and he's taken all his things with him.'

'There's no sign of him out here. I'll grab a torch and head down to the gate. He can't have gone very far.'

'Let me come with you,' she begged, cursing herself for not keeping tabs on him when he'd been so upset. Katherine had told her she'd need eyes in the back of her head to watch the children but she'd seized the quiet to wallow, not realising it had been the calm before the storm.

'Not unless you put on some warm clothes first.'

Iona complied without fuss, fetching her coat and shoes before meeting him again at the door.

'We'll lock the door behind us and if we don't find Hamish soon, you come back here and I'll carry on the search myself.' Fraser handed her a torch and pre-empted her fears about leaving a second child alone.

Hamish would never have entertained the idea of leaving the comfort of the house to venture out into the wilderness if he'd been happy, and she was accountable for his current state of mind regardless of anything Fraser said to the contrary.

'Hamish!'

Every now and then they caught a glimpse of beady eyes watching from the edge of the trees, which turned out to be woodland creatures curious about who else was out here with them. With each crunch of the undergrowth in the distance, every creepy sound of forest wildlife, she drew closer and closer to Fraser's side, sure he'd protect her from any assailant who might come from the shadows. Goodness knew how a small boy was coping out here when a grown woman was letting her imagination scare her half to death.

'What was that?'

'It's an owl.'

'Did you hear that? Anything could be lurking out here.'

'It's the countryside, Iona. You have to expect some noise from the neighbours. We are sharing their habitat after all.' Fraser was right, she'd been brought up in the city with a soundtrack of speeding cars and emergency sirens, not living, breathing creatures. Unless you counted the drunks who had sometimes serenaded her outside her bedroom window. This relative peace took some getting used to.

'What are we going to do when we find him, Fraser?' *If* wasn't an option. They had to find him but they also had to get him to come back with them and to want to stay with them. Otherwise social services would have to get involved and it was disheartening to think Hamish would rather do that than spend another night under the same roof as them.

'Get him into the heat as soon as possible before he ends up with hypothermia, tell him off for scaring us, then have a talk about the position we've all been put in.'

'How come you're so sensible about all this?' Fraser was managing this all so much better than she was and more than she'd given him credit for. Anyone would think he'd had experience in caring for children it came so naturally to him. The total opposite of the father figure and domineering partner she'd assumed he'd make.

'It might be difficult for you to accept but I was a boy once too. One who found himself in a similar situation. Except my parents chose to send me away to live with strangers.' The explanation didn't make it sound any less heartless. Unlike Katherine, his parents had had a choice. It was gut-wrenching to picture any child in that predicament but more so of Fraser as that lost little soul when he was such a source of strength to her now.

Iona had been afraid and unhappy too but she'd had her mother to remind her she was wanted and loved, even if her parents hadn't demonstrated it to each other. It was no wonder he gave off that defensive vibe that made it difficult to get close to him. She counted herself lucky he'd let her see the real Fraser, who was warm and caring and everything his parents apparently hadn't been for him. Instead of launching herself at him and forcing a hug on him, she cleared the ache in her throat and simply said, 'Childhood sucks.'

'But it makes us who we are today. You want to know why I'm such a stickler for the rules and doing everything by the book? It's because I thought, by being the perfect son, my parents might love me more and want me around. I thought I'd been too wild, too unruly for them to have at home. Clinging to the rules, projecting that perfect image in the hope people will like me has become my way of life. I don't know why when it's never worked.' He gave a bitter laugh but there was nothing remotely funny about what he'd shared with her.

Iona knew that kind of loneliness and uncertainly intimately, along with that constant worry about trying to please people who neither deserved nor appreciated it. Yet, since coming here with the children, she'd never had any sense he'd been pretending to be anyone else other than himself. It might be because he'd abandoned his rule book for their sakes.

It was proof of his strength that he'd become such a success yet had retained that compassion that endeared him to his patients, and now her too. A lesser mortal might have rebelled against the idea of school and authority but Fraser had turned it to his advantage and applied it to his career to get him to the position of senior practice partner. Every day revealed new layers to Dr McColl, making it impossible for her to deny her growing affection for him. The longer they were under the same roof, the closer they became physically and emotionally. It was lucky they had two small children to act as a buffer between them. As long as they remained safe, she was sure her heart would too.

'Listen. Do you hear that?' Fraser stopped beside her.

'Don't you start. I thought I was the paranoid one here.'

'Shh. Listen.'

She was about to tear strips off him for shushing her when she heard the faint cry for herself. They stood motionless, holding their breath, hoping to locate the source.

'Help.'

The plaintive cry was so full of pain and exhaustion she cursed the McColl family for not having the foresight to install floodlights out here for such emergencies.

'Hamish? Where are you?' Fraser's voice carried easily through the night, ensuring the boy would hear it no matter which direction he was in.

'At the gate.'

They sprinted the last few yards to reach him, their torch beams picking out a crumpled figure lying on the other side of the metalwork. Iona clamped her hand over her mouth to smother her gasp. 'What on earth happened? How did you end up down there?'

'He's tried to climb over the gate.' Fraser jabbed the security code into the control panel and they waited for an eternity for the gates to open and allow them access to the child.

'Where did you think you were going out here?' Iona knelt down beside him and brushed the dirt from his face, glad to see him again.

'I want to see my mum.' Hamish's face was streaked with tears and mud and Iona had to catch her own sob before it escaped with his.

'Can you stand?' Fraser was focused on the injuries Hamish had sustained during his not-so-great escape. Shock was probably the least he'd be suffering from the height he'd fallen.

Hamish sat up and Fraser attempted to disentangle the backpack from around his shoulders only to prompt an ear-piercing scream.

'My arm hurts so bad.' The unearthly squeals subsided into equally disturbing whimpers. Each agonising sound was like a fist in the gut. Hamish would never have been hurt if Iona had come home as planned.

'He might have broken it.' Fraser tossed her the backpack and scooped the boy up into his arms, careful not to jar the arm he was cradling.

It wasn't a life or death emergency but they took him back to the house with no less urgency, guided by one torch now that Fraser had his hands full.

'The key is in my pocket.' He turned to her in the porch lights and she stuck her hand in to fumble for it, trying not to acknowledge the solid muscled thighs beneath her fingertips.

Once back in the house Fraser laid Hamish gently on the sofa and Iona switched on every light and lamp she could find so they could examine him.

'We're going to have to get your coat off so I can check that arm, Hamish.' Fraser didn't want to hurt him any more than he already had been, but he had to assess the damage to prevent further injury. Hamish was responsive and breathing and Fraser didn't want to think about what could've happened if they hadn't found him out there.

Hamish wasn't his son but after a couple of days of taking care of him Fraser worried just the same. It was impossible not to draw comparisons with his own parents and their apparent lack of compassion for their only child when the severity of Hamish's injuries was taking priority right now.

Iona put her hand to the boy's back to help him upright and between them they managed to remove his outer layer with the minimum of discomfort. Hamish peeled his sleeve back to expose the skin, every whimper reminding him this was more than a scratch. Although Hamish's complexion was grey from the shock, there was no blood and the bone hadn't broken the skin, minimising the risk of infection.

Fraser confirmed that Hamish could move his fingers with no sign of numbness or blue tinge to suggest otherwise. The swelling, bruising and tenderness around the deformed area he was protecting so vehemently did, however, suggest a fracture of some description.

'I think you've broken your arm, Hamish. We need to stabilise it here, support it so there won't be any further damage done until we get you to the emergency department.'

'It hurts.' The fear and pain wasn't just from Hamish's arm—it was clearly also about not having either of his parents here to comfort him when he needed them.

'They'll put a cast on it at the hospital, you know.' Iona leaned over the back of the couch, trying to find a silver lining in this for him.

'They will?' Hamish stopped crying to mull that over.

It occurred to Fraser that those unfortunates who had come to school with broken bones encased in plaster had suddenly become the most popular pupils there. 'Yeah, and everyone will want to sign it.'

Fraser winked at Iona for her quick thinking as it could keep Hamish distracted from his injury for a while and get him to co-operate.

'Will it hurt?' he asked, narrowing his eyes, suspicious they were conspiring against him.

'Not at all. They'll just want to protect your arm. As I do.'

'I think your mum packed some liquid paracetamol for you so that should help with the pain. Fraser, do you have ice in your freezer to bring that swelling down?' Iona, satisfied that Hamish was going to let them help, took the first step to stabilising the injured limb.

'Yes. Top drawer. You'll find towels and tape in the bathroom.' Fraser was going to have to improvise a splint for the journey. There were a lot of household items they could utilise, such as rolled-up newspapers, but towels would provide some padding and relieve some of the discomfort.

'Hang in there, pal, we'll hit the road as soon as we get that arm supported.

'Then I can visit my mum?' Whether this injury had been a deliberate attempt to get Hamish to his mother, or an unfortunate coincidence as he'd tried to run to her, there was no question of his desperation to see her.

'I'll see what I can do.' Fraser couldn't bring himself to be angry about it. If he'd had an inkling his parents would've welcomed the sight of him at any given moment he'd have broken out of boarding school in a heartbeat.

Before Fraser was forced into making any promises that might be beyond his ability to carry out, Iona returned with supplies.

'Would you believe Poppy's still fast asleep?' She shook her head as she deposited the ice, towels, bandages and tape on the coffee table and administered a spoonful of medicine to Hamish for the pain.

'Thank goodness for small mercies.' With the smallest one of them safe and sound, they could concentrate on the one they'd failed. Parenting was hard and they weren't perfect by any means but the important thing was they were doing their best.

With some manoeuvring and cajoling they managed to get Hamish to lay his arm down on the folded towel, covering the distance from his fingertips to slightly past his elbow. Fraser tied the towel around the arm, making sure it was completely wrapped and snug, tied at either end and avoiding any pressure on the injury site.

'Can you wiggle your fingertips for me?' He rechecked circulation, sensation and motion to make sure he hadn't tied it too tight but the arm remained immobilised.

When Fraser was satisfied Hamish was as comfortable as could be expected, Iona fashioned a sling from the bandage to cradle his arm, fastening it around his neck to make it secure.

'That's not too tight, is it?' she queried before backing off.

'Thanks.' Fraser could've handled this on his own but it was reassuring to have her here, backing him up. They were a team, and for the first time in forever he no longer felt alone. This was how he imagined a family would be, all pulling together to make life more than bearable for one another. He wasn't looking forward to the time when Iona and the kids moved out and he was back to rattling around the house on his own with no one to think about but himself. It did much more for the soul to be around people, helping when and where he could.

Iona draped Hamish's coat around his shoulders, presumably to stave off some of the cold facing them on the other side of the front door.

'If you're happy to stay here with Poppy, I'll drive Hamish myself.' It wasn't that he wanted to leave her but it was more practical than waking the little girl to make the long journey Iona had already done once today.

'Sure. Let me know that you've got there safely.' That made him smile. He wasn't used to having someone worry about him and to know he'd impacted on her in some small way meant the world to him.

'I will.'

It wasn't easy getting Hamish into the back of the car but eventually they got the seat belt around him so it wasn't jarring his forearm. He had more colour in his cheeks now and he'd stopped whimpering. In fact, he was having trouble staying awake, so the car ride could put him over into sleep soon.

'I'm sure you're exhausted after the day you've had. Get yourself to bed and we'll let ourselves back in. Whatever time that might be.'

With the car door closed on Hamish to keep the wind off him, they were left facing each other in the driveway.

'I'm sure yours has been equally as eventful. Thanks for taking him. Just make sure you take care.'

'I will,' he assured her. He had a lot to come back for.

Iona threw her arms around him for a hug and kissed him on the lips as though she was afraid she'd never see him again.

Fraser embraced the contact, catching her around the waist and finally admitting to himself that he was fast falling for her. He lost himself in the kiss, fuelled with the desire which had been rising in him for days.

Her warm mouth on his, her tongue seeking his, turned the goodbye peck into passionate foreplay. There was nothing he wanted more than to sweep her up in his arms and carry her off to his bedroom and close the door on the rest of the world but it would have to wait. They had responsibilities and he wasn't the sort of man who'd put his wants before the needs of a child.

With great reluctance Fraser pulled back while he could still think straight, rested his forehead against hers and waited for the white noise in his head to subside.

'I'll see you when I get back.' His voice was thick with emotions he'd long thought dormant.

They extricated their limbs from each other until they were only holding on by their fingertips and they finally had to let go or he'd never get in the car.

Kissing Iona went against all the restrictions he'd imposed in order to protect his heart. Yet it was one of the best moves he'd ever made.

He set off for the distant city lights with a spark of hope in his soul that he might not be alone for the rest of his days after all. Unlike the little boy so often shunned by his parents and the adult orphan forced to return to the ancestral home alone, Fraser was finally excited about coming back. That was down to Iona being there and for once he didn't want to have his future all laid out for him. It excited him more to wait and see what could happen.

Iona stumbled back to the house in a daze and gave one last wave at Fraser driving away before going back inside. She touched her fingers to her softly swollen lips, which were throbbing from Fraser's tender kiss. For days they'd been fighting that recurring desire for each other but there was no denying it was there and she had no will to fight it any more either.

On a day when everything had gone wrong, Fraser had ended it on a high for her. Who knew where that kiss would lead to? But she wanted more. Now she was convinced he wasn't the prison jailer she'd assumed him to be there was no reason to keep her feelings for him on ice.

Deep down she'd known he was nothing like Andy even before he'd shared the painful truth behind his need for order in his life. It was his security blanket, as her solitude was hers. These past days, however, had shown her it was no longer enough to simply exist in her safe bubble and to really embrace her new life she had to let someone step inside it with her. She could honestly say so far that living with Fraser had only been positive and those long-held fears about allowing a man to get close to her again were beginning to ebb.

Fraser knew she wasn't a woman who could be pushed around and he seemed to respect that, making her fears about repeating past mistakes redundant. The timing was awkward but a relationship shouldn't affect the children if they kept it quiet. They were going to have enough on their plates anyway with the aftermath of Hamish's exploits.

Not only were there physical restrictions on him now but they were going to have to explain the accident to his mother.

She groaned. It would be a miracle if Katherine agreed to let her continue as his interim guardian after this.

Once she'd peeked in on their younger, less troublesome charge again, Iona stripped the pillows and cover off her bed and brought them downstairs.

With the lounge curtains slightly parted she'd be able to see the others coming back from her makeshift bed on the sofa. Fraser's ancestors wouldn't have approved but the man himself would only want her to be happy and that seemed to overrule his sense of decorum these days. A quality she simply couldn't find fault with, regardless of how hard she'd tried to.

CHAPTER NINE

IT WAS THE early hours of the morning before the travellers returned. Outside it was dark and gloomy, the kind of winter morning when you didn't want to get out of bed, even if it was only a blanket on a sofa. Iona wouldn't have been surprised if Fraser had decided not to drive back until the sun came up but now that she could stop fretting about him falling asleep at the wheel, her tension headache was easing off.

Iona had managed a couple of hours' sleep but she couldn't say they'd been particularly restful, on alert for Poppy upstairs and the sound of the car coming back outside. Not to mention the adrenaline pumping around her body in anticipation of embarking on a new phase of her life with Fraser. Bit by bit he was helping her see relationships didn't have to be toxic. She could have someone by her side, enriching her life with support instead of trying to snuff out her spirit. Perhaps in time she'd get to do the same for him and show him he deserved to be loved for exactly who he was.

Fraser stepped out of the car looking as spritely and alert as if he'd had a full eight hours' sleep and opened the rear car door to emerge with a sleeping Hamish in his arms. Iona smoothed down the crumpled clothes she'd slept in and tried to tame the nest of snakes she called her hair before she ran to the door.

'Is he okay?' she whispered, spying the cast covering most of his forearm.

'He'll be fine.' Despite the possibility he must be running on empty, Fraser summoned the energy to flash her a reassuring smile. Iona couldn't believe she'd ever believed this man to be selfish when he'd shown her a hundred different ways how wrong she'd been, setting his own comfort aside to give them all whatever they needed at any given time. Other than her mother, she'd never known anyone else to do that for her and it comforted her knowing she wouldn't be on her own with whatever the next crisis was.

Out of the blue it occurred to her he'd make a great father one day and made her wonder why he wasn't one already. He had a successful career, a title and an estate, he was drop-dead gorgeous and a natural with children. Unless he had some horrible, dark secret locked away in the cellar, she couldn't understand why his ex hadn't snatched him up, having fallen madly in love with him. A few days in his company and Iona knew she was well on the way there herself.

Perhaps it was his childhood experiences preventing him from settling down. She could empathise when her knowledge of parenting had come from two people who should never have stayed together. Both she and Fraser had to figure out who they were in their own right, away from the influences of the past.

She watched him carry Hamish to bed, her blood pumping so fast in her veins as she acknowledged those strong feelings there was every chance she might pass out. The man was carrying a sleeping child to bed after driving for hours so she could get some rest. Andy had never shown her such consideration from the day they'd married. The problem was she and Fraser had gone past the point where a quick fling would satisfy, too involved in each other's lives now for anything casual. If they acted on that kiss, picked up from where they'd left off, she had no doubt it would be the start of something so serious and meaningful it made the hairs stand up on the back of her neck. Yet she was intrigued by the possibility of something new and exciting to spice up her life.

To take her mind off the shock at the new direction things had suddenly taken, and wanting to thank Fraser, Iona set about making some breakfast in the kitchen. She lifted out some eggs and bacon and proceeded to cook them while waiting for the toast to pop and the kettle to boil. This house had been designed and built to be an intimidating status symbol, yet Fraser had made her feel part of it and she was no longer afraid of breaking something or forgetting proper protocol. There'd been a marked change in Fraser's behaviour since they'd moved in and it showed how hard he was working to overcome his hang-ups rather than force them all to conform. Something she appreciated to a level he couldn't possibly understand.

'Something smells good.'

Iona's stomach flipped along with the bacon and eggs at the sound of Fraser's voice and she wondered how they were going to be able to work together again when she went gooey inside every time he spoke.

Viewing the scene through the eyes of a third party, it could be construed as the very picture of domesticity, sharing a quiet breakfast together after a rough night with the kids, and she couldn't find a thing wrong with it.

'I'm starving. All I had was a curled-up sandwich from the vending machine and the dregs left in the coffee machine. It's so nice to come home to a cooked meal and good company.'

The compliment was likely born primarily from his

hunger but Iona knew herself it was much preferable to returning to an empty flat and a microwaveable meal for one.

'So, no complications with Hamish's arm?' Normally she'd refrain from bringing up medical matters at the table but he was a doctor and wouldn't be as squeamish as the average person.

'A small fracture. It should heal in no time.'

'That's good news, I suppose. We'll still have to tell Katherine about it, though.' It wouldn't say much for their ability to take care of her children if Hamish had broken his arm already and Iona wouldn't blame her if she decided to discharge herself to do the job properly herself.

'It's all sorted,' Fraser said once he'd swallowed his huge bite of toast. 'I managed to sneak Hamish in to see her while we were there.'

'How on earth did you manage that? On second thoughts, maybe I don't want to know.' It wouldn't take much for a handsome doctor to sweet talk his way in anywhere and she didn't want to hear the details of him charming some other woman who wasn't her.

'Katherine was awake, she's still not sleeping, so I explained what had happened. She understood, had a chat with Hamish and he's promised to behave. He's much happier now he's seen his mum.'

'I'm glad. I trust you told her how sorry we are?' The development lessened the burden of guilt lying heavily upon her.

'I did and it only succeeded in making her cry and thanking us again for taking them on.' Fraser shrugged then proceeded to clear his plate and drain his cup.

'I suppose you'll want to get some sleep?' After last night they were all entitled to a lie-in. Everything else could wait until they had clear heads again to think about where they were headed next.

'I managed a nap when Hamish was getting X-rayed

but I'm probably better staying up now or I'll end up with night-lag. Actually, I was thinking about Christmas here.'

'Oh?' In all of yesterday's drama Iona had forgotten about the very event she'd been building up to and which she'd done a very poor job of preparing for so far. Unforgiveable for someone who'd promised not only herself but two young children she'd make the Yuletide special.

'I think we need a make-over. Especially with Hamish. Perhaps if we give them Christmas we could all learn to forgive and forget the mistakes of the past twenty-four hours.'

'What do you suggest?' He'd obviously been concocting some sort of plan to bring it up now.

'Well…' He shifted in his seat, appearing restless to get on with it as soon as possible. 'Christmas here was never the jolly family fun time most people associate with the season. Even when my parents did deign to bring me home for it, we merely went through the motions. I always knew their heart wasn't in it but that doesn't mean we didn't decorate accordingly. The house made a picture-perfect Christmas-card scene if it didn't go beyond the superficial exterior.' His description of his strained family time tugged at her heartstrings for the young Fraser who'd been denied a childhood.

The way he'd looked after her and the children made it clear he was someone who had so much love to give and deserved buckets of it in return. To feel unwanted, unloved and confused by what was going on in the adult world around him must have been frightening for him. Each time he did something to make them feel safe here, Iona knew it was because he wished someone had been around to do the same for him at that age. For all the money and land he'd been surrounded by, his life sounded as lonely and messed up as hers had been and the emotional damage done in those formative years wasn't easy to shake off even as an adult. They had more in common than anyone would've guessed from their vastly different backgrounds.

'In that case, what are we waiting for?' Iona was wide awake again and ready to get started now he'd put the thought in her head that they might actually be having their first proper Christmas. Together.

After all he'd been through, Fraser was offering so much by opening his home to them and Iona wanted to show him the best of the season along with the children. It would have been easier for him to lock himself away here on his own for the holidays, the way she'd planned to. Or, worse, taken out his pain and dislike of Christmas on those around him. He was better than that, stronger, and if he was prepared to stand up and reclaim his life back from fear, it gave her the impetus to do the same.

Opening the door to the attic made Fraser's heart pound just as much now as it had when he'd been a bairn. That creak giving away his location to anyone who happened to be searching for him, that blast of cold air bringing goose-bumps to his skin and the dust filling his nostrils as he disturbed the family mausoleum of memories.

The only time he'd been up here as an adult had been shortly after his father had passed away to store boxes of his personal papers and belongings until he decided what to do with them. He'd been alone then, Caroline playing no part in his actions then, when Iona was the very reason he was up here now.

'Watch your step. There isn't much light up here, I'm afraid. We didn't spend much time in this part of the house.' Fraser took Iona's hand in his and guided her steps with the aid of the single light bulb hanging in the middle of the vast space. A scary place for a child with a vivid imagination. Scarier still for a grown man who hadn't fully dealt with his father's death and the unanswered questions he'd left behind.

Once she was on a firm footing he had to let go of her hand even though he liked the feel of it there, soft and warm and comforting that he wasn't here alone.

'Where should we start?' With her sleeves rolled up, Iona was gung-ho about tracking down these vintage decorations he'd told her were here. Hands on hips, ready to excavate, she could've been standing at the entrance of a pharaoh's tomb, ready to create history, she exuded such excitement. It was refreshing to see her embrace that inner child when he'd gagged and bound his long ago.

The contrast of her exuberance in the midst of this stuffy environment helped Fraser see it was possible for the two to exist together here. If anything, her sense of freedom brightened the whole house and Fraser wondered if by stifling his childish enthusiasm back then he hadn't done his family a disservice. Perhaps if he'd been allowed, by his parents and himself, to explore the boundaries more he could have brought light into the place to combat the sombre spectre of his mother's illness.

He kicked out at one of the boxes but there was nothing could be done now to salvage his relationship with his parents. All he could do was focus on those people who were important in his life now.

'What about here?' He headed to the far side of the room where neatly stacked boxes were labelled for convenience. An act he doubted either of his parents had undertaken. His father would've deemed such manual work demeaning to a man of his standing, and his mother had never ventured far from her bed for much of his childhood. Yet he recognised her handwriting on the containers, tracing his fingers over her elegant letters and wondering when she'd handed over responsibility to the staff instead of sharing it with her only child.

'Let's see what we've got,' Fraser said, dismantling the tower to place the boxes side by side on the patchwork carpet underfoot, comprised of offcuts and old rugs his father had refused to throw out.

'May I?' Iona sat cross-legged in the midst of the display, itching to unwrap whatever treasures she imagined they'd find.

'Go for it.' Fraser didn't have any sentimentality for any of this stuff and if he needed the space he wouldn't think twice about getting rid of everything. If they could fulfil one promise to the children, though, and create the sort of wonderland Iona had envisaged all along, he was willing to finally sort through it. With the children fast asleep in their beds they had plenty of time to do it.

It had been on his mind the whole way to the hospital and back to do something that would lift everyone's spirits. After all, they'd all been orphaned in one way or another for the holidays. As the adults, it was down to him and Iona to make the place feel like less of a foster home when none of them had planned to be here.

Of course, that hadn't been the only thing on his mind. Kissing Iona had ensured he stayed awake and alert for the entire journey. He didn't know why he'd done it any more than why he'd brought her up here with him.

Only that it felt right. There'd been no faking the concern she'd shown for Hamish when he'd gone missing, or her willingness to co-operate with him when it had been desperately needed. No more reason to keep hiding from his growing feelings for her.

'These are beautiful.' Iona reverently unwrapped a box of vintage baubles, each decorated with snowy scenes on their fragile glass shells.

'We should have a tree somewhere to hang them on.' Behind another stack of boxes he eventually found the artificial Christmas tree that, at some point, had replaced the real pine they'd once picked out together.

Flashing images of those times flickered at the back of his mind when they'd been happy, together as a family, which he'd long forgotten. He couldn't figure out if it was better or worse to discover the atmosphere around the season hadn't always been as strained as he remembered in those early days before it had turned into such a chore for all of them.

'Your handiwork, I presume?' Iona dangled a pipe-cleaner reindeer complete with googly eyes and a tiny red pom-pom nose from her finger, delighted with her find.

Fraser took the handmade decoration and stretched out beside her, fighting back the emotion suddenly trying to burn a hole in his chest. 'I remember making this with Mum.'

He pulled up his legs and laid the reindeer on his knees to see it better.

'You did have some good times with her, then?'

'When I was very small—I hardly remember—I think we used to have craft days. We made silly animals and space rockets out of whatever she had in this big wooden art chest. It was full of cards and stickers and glitter, and all sorts.' The memories came flooding back, almost drowning him with images of them playing together, actually going out as a family, his mother and father either side of him, swinging him by both arms and laughter ringing out all around.

'That's lovely, Fraser. She sounds as though she really loved you.'

'At one time. Then she got sick and no one seemed to want me around any more. After she died, well, Dad was old-fashioned and he didn't know how to raise a child on his own, he'd left all of that to Mum. I suppose it was easier to let the masters at boarding school do his job for him but we were never close again. He paid my school fees and put me through medical school but we were more acquaintances than father and son.' Tears were burning the backs of his eyeballs for that boy once surrounded by love who had somehow ended up abandoned miles from home and for the relationships he'd lost with his parents.

He spotted a rare family photograph lying at the bottom of the box and lifted it out. It had been taken at Christmas, these same decorations hanging downstairs in the background. He couldn't have been any older than Poppy—it was before he'd been sent away from home. They were all smiling, opening presents under the tree like any other normal family. Fraser's insides flipped over at the sight. There were probably no other happy snaps of them together after that and with both parents now gone there wouldn't be another.

Fraser could feel the warmth of the tears falling down his face but he didn't wipe them away, finally letting the emotions of the past run free. It was Iona who softly brushed away the evidence of his pain, stroking his face and giving him the comfort he desperately needed.

'Is it possible they might have sent you away because they thought they were protecting you in some way from your mother's illness? Neither of us can know for sure what their reasons were but when I look at that photograph and hear how much your mother loved spending time with you it does make me wonder if they thought it was best for you. We both know the toll cancer takes on a family and they might not have wanted you to watch her decline.' Iona clasped both of his hands in hers, trying to make him look back on the time from an adult standpoint instead of as that confused little boy.

He'd blocked out those happier times because he'd had tunnel vision about being to blame for being sent away. Deep down he must have known they'd loved him at one time but he'd spent more of his life with stern strangers so those memories had gradually faded. The only vivid recollections he'd had were the traumatic ones because they'd had such an emotional impact on him. Perhaps he'd perceived the separation from his parents as neglect because he'd been angry at them for leaving him.

It wasn't surprising he'd become an afterthought to his parents with the surgeries and treatments that had gone hand in hand with the breast cancer and the later, secondary cancers that had spread throughout his mother's body.

This new theory that they'd tried to protect him, not cause him pain, didn't lighten his heart, only made him sad for the time with his parents stolen from him. These days they would have had counselling, talked through their feelings and had other help to pull them through the sickness and bereavement. Instead, illness had devastated the whole family piece by piece, the same way cancer had taken his mother. It was such a waste.

'I suppose it's possible but it can't change what happened or how I felt.'

'Can't you find it in your heart to forgive them?' Iona rested her forehead against his, their hands still clutched together between their chests.

'I can try.' Fraser didn't want to hold on to a grudge or remain trapped in this guilt any longer. It would be time and energy better spent focused on the future.

'It might help you find some closure. I know it sounds hypocritical when I've come out here to escape the people who were supposed to love me most in the world. I lost my mother too but my father's still alive. I can't say he ever showed me any such affection. If he had I might think more kindly towards him and might not have let myself get swept up into an abusive relationship myself.'

Fraser knew how much her experiences must have impacted on her given that he was still in recovery from his last break-up. But Iona had been married, physically hurt by the man she'd intended to spend her whole life with, and that wasn't something easily forgotten.

'You're the strongest woman I've ever met.' While he'd remained locked in the house with his resentment and anger, Iona had moved on and somehow managed to leave the issues of her early life behind to focus on her future. Not only that, she'd devoted herself to helping others and proving she was better than the man who'd claimed to be her father.

'I've had to be. I don't have anyone else.' She turned away from him and busied herself with putting the decorations back in the box, including his prized reindeer, but she didn't fool him. That tough façade was protecting a fragile heart identical to his.

'Hey.' He caught her chin between his thumb and finger and turned her head so he could drop a soft kiss on her lips to let her know he wasn't going anywhere. 'You've got me.'

'Have I, Fraser? I don't want to get into something I'm going to regret. Do you promise you're going to be here for me?' The question was so full of residual pain he knew she couldn't bear to have it inflicted on her again.

Right here, talking about and raking through the remnants of his past with her, the wind rattling the old bones of this house, it was the only place he wanted to be. She'd messed up yesterday but she'd owned it, wanted to make amends, and that was more than anyone who'd wronged him in the past had ever done. Being with Iona, he didn't have to think about the next step, free to do whatever came naturally without fear of being judged.

He was beginning to see what Caroline had meant when she'd accused him of not being true to her, or himself, when he'd been unwittingly projecting an image of the man he imagined he *should* be, instead of the one he was around Iona. He needed to embrace every part of who he was to fully enjoy life, including that inner child who'd been stifled for too long. He had nothing to lose and everything to gain.

'Always,' he promised, and kissed her again. It was the sweet reward he'd been waiting for since last night, the thought of which had got him to the hospital and back without incident, knowing she'd be at home, waiting for him.

He felt her soften at his touch then she kissed him back with such urgency and desire he didn't want to think about anyone other than the woman back in his arms where she belonged.

He shifted her onto his lap, never breaking the seal between their mouths because he couldn't get enough of her. She unbuttoned her blouse and Fraser helped tug it over her head to reveal her full breasts cupped in wisps of black lace. Every part of his body tightened to attention, begging to be freed with her.

He pulled off his sweater and Iona stood up to remove the rest of her clothes, leaving her breathtakingly naked before him. He barely had a chance to drink in the beautiful sight or unzip his trousers before she straddled him again and lowered herself onto his straining erection.

The immediacy of the act jolted him, body and soul, every nerve ending ready to explode with satisfaction. The intimacy wasn't purely physical as they stared into each other's eyes, rocking together in search of that place of utter peace. They needed each other, needed to find a release for all of those pent-up emotions and replace the pain with something much more enjoyable.

Iona bore down on his shoulders, riding him with relentless urgency, her breasts bouncing as Fraser thrust ever upwards to meet her. He caught her tight, pink nipple in his mouth, sucking hard enough to make her gasp and contract her inner muscles around his shaft. The sensation urged him on to tease the other pinched bud but she arched her back, increased the pace of her hip grinding and drove him to the brink of insanity much too quickly.

With one swift movement he flipped over so she was on her back and he was deep inside her, his movements no longer restricted between her thighs. Unencumbered, he drove deeper and harder inside her, Iona lifting her hips to accommodate every inch of him. Bodies slamming together, Iona's nails clawing his back, each of them making those animalistic noises that only came with raw passion, Fraser knew they were out of control. Neither of them held back about what it was they wanted, or demanded, from each other.

He prided himself on being a considerate lover, aiming to please his partner as much as himself. Yet, with Iona, he was acting on pure, carnal instinct. As she was. At the end of this no one would be left wanting.

Iona knew exactly what she wanted, him, and he was more than happy to oblige. Their chemistry hadn't been a figment of his imagination when they were living out the hot, frenzied truth of it together.

As the wind picked up outside, so too did the ferocity of their coupling. Iona's moans grew more frequent and higher pitched, her muscles tightening to let him know she was almost at breaking point. With every bit of strength he had in him, Fraser drove into her again and again and pushed her over the edge, tumbling with her into that all-enveloping ecstasy of release.

He'd never lost himself so utterly with a woman before and he knew this was more than great sex or physical attraction. It was love for who she was, how she made him feel, and who he was when he was with her. The sort of connection a man was lucky to find once in a lifetime and would be a fool to ever let go.

* * *

Iona curled her naked body around Fraser's, certain that was all the activity she was capable of for the foreseeable future. He'd reached parts of her she hadn't known still existed, the most significant of which had been her heart. Sure, this was, and would probably remain for a long time, the most erotic and passionate encounter of her life but she wanted this to be the start of something between them, not simply the culmination of all the drama and emotion they'd been dealing with.

Fraser had shared a lot with her, including those poignant memories of his parents. Then there was all the passion she'd somehow unlocked from within him. She shivered, the feel of him so new, so recent and so very pleasurable.

'Are you cold?' He mistook her goosebumps for something entirely different and wrapped his arms and legs around her to share his body heat. She wasn't about to complain. This was the most content she'd been in an age and if it wasn't for their sleeping babes downstairs she'd happily stay locked in here for the rest of the day.

Every now and then Fraser kissed the top of her head, reassuring her he was there, all the while she was wondering if he'd become distant, lost in his thoughts. She was confident that he wasn't regretting the tryst but if there was something else bothering him she wanted to put his mind at rest.

'I...er... I'm on the Pill. Thought you should know.' In her line of work she'd seen plenty of women caught out by the same rush of lust causing them to lose common sense and gain a surprise bundle nine months later not to take precautions herself. Although she'd never been so carried away before that the idea of contraception had never entered her head. Fraser wasn't the sort to overlook something as important as protection either but apparently the buttoned-up Dr McColl was just as hot-blooded as the next male. More so, judging by her limited experience.

'Oh. Right. Good. Sorry. I should've taken care of that.' His embarrassment at being ill prepared was as obvious as the fact that wasn't the subject monopolising his thoughts.

'Is there something wrong? You seem so far away.' She rolled onto his chest so she could look into his face and see for herself if he was having second thoughts about getting involved. It wasn't in her nature, or her plans, to be the needy, clingy girlfriend. She simply preferred to know where she stood. There was nothing to be gained for either of them by embarking on another sham of a relationship.

'I'm right here.' He deliberately misinterpreted her comment and tried to distract her with another one of his swoonworthy kisses, which, although gratifying all the way down to her toes, didn't answer her question.

She let him distract her a while longer, until she was in danger of not caring about what had snagged his attention as much as the new yearning he was awakening inside her.

In between smooches and desperately pretending she hadn't noticed the hand tangled in her hair and the one caressing her breast, she asked the question again.

'Where did you go, Fraser?' *Without me*, she wanted to add.

She lifted her head off his chest as he drew in a ragged breath.

'I was just thinking...the kids will be up soon.' He wasn't telling her the whole truth but he was back in the present with her and thinking about the future. Even if it was only the immediate one.

'I know but I don't want to move.' She drew her fingernail around his nipple, teasing the sensitive skin and watching it pucker with arousal.

'Neither do I but we, uh, came up here for a reason.' He grabbed her hand and gave her a half-hearted scolding, his

ever-darkening eyes and swiftly recovering libido telling
her what he'd much rather be doing. Unfortunately, he was
all about doing the right thing, not always necessarily the
most fun thing, but on this occasion she had to concede he
was right. They'd had their quality time together, which, if
all went well, they'd get to repeat somewhere more comfortable and at a more convenient time. That didn't give
her any more motivation to move.

'Spoilsport. Don't you have house elves who come in
and do all the work while you're asleep?'

'We call them staff, sweetheart, and, as you know, I
don't employ any here. It doesn't sit well with my conscience.'

'Damn you and your principles. With one ring of a bell
we could've summoned someone to bring us a bed up here
and sent a nanny downstairs to see to the children.' She
burrowed further into Fraser's side.

His chuckling eventually ended with an abrupt 'Up!',
and her clothes landing item by item on top of her naked
body. There was something sexy about when he was being
bossy, especially when he was naked and she'd had experience of what it was like letting him be on top.

For once she did as he asked.

CHAPTER TEN

IONA HAD A renewed burst of energy once they'd transported their festive finds down to the living room. Running on pure adrenaline since she'd had next to no sleep, she set to work creating a sophisticated winter wonderland as much for Fraser as the children.

He might not have been invested in the aesthetic design but she set him to work where his height was an advantage.

'Hang that garland from the ceiling...

'Drape that bunting around the lintel...

'Find somewhere to put the mistletoe...'

That last instruction drew a lascivious grin from her co-worker as he held the plastic spray somewhere that would make a Christmas angel blush. 'I think custom dictates you're supposed to kiss me under this.'

He'd grown bolder now they'd shared intimate knowledge of one another but she knew he was joking. For now. The next time they had the place to themselves she'd call his bluff and kiss him everywhere south of his impressive sprig.

'You wish.' She tossed some tinsel at him and set his mind back to the task rather than the contents of his trousers. Although that was easier said than done for her too.

'Wow! Did you do all this while we were sleeping?' An

animated Hamish walking in on them soon extinguished all explicit thoughts circulating in the atmosphere.

'Iona did most of it. What do you think?' Fraser credited her with the display when it had been his idea to work through the morning in an attempt to get her back into their good books.

'It's cool. Thanks.' Hamish was back to being the good-natured boy they'd first met, thanks to Fraser's uncharacteristic bending of the rules at the hospital. She trusted he was beginning to see the benefits of acting on instinct and not always following the rules. Making love on his attic floor wouldn't have been scheduled into his daily planner and it was all the more memorable for it.

'It's so pretty.' Poppy came to stand beside her at the tree, marvelling at the delicate baubles and tartan bows.

'Do you want to put the fairy on the top of the tree?' Iona handed over her favourite task to the bleary-eyed child in her pink pyjamas, imagining her mother doing the same thing with her every year.

The McColl fairy was altogether different from the Munro one, which was a chubby-cheeked, soft-bodied angel. She wore scarlet felt trimmed with gold and berries instead of white netting and Poppy was enchanted with her as she placed her carefully on the tree.

'Look! It's snowing.' They all followed Poppy's gaze out of the window to see snowflakes falling like confetti outside. It was the perfect backdrop to their Christmas scene but the snow was always more welcomed by children than the adults. Especially out here where there were no road gritters to clear a path for people who had to get to work in a hurry. Thank goodness they had no plans today beyond keeping the children entertained.

'Can we go out and play?' Hamish had his nose pressed up against the glass with longing.

'After breakfast. What would you like?' Fraser took a

turn at being the grown-up and temporarily put the fun and games on hold.

Poppy tugged on his jumper. 'Can we have pancakes?' she asked, as tentatively as though she'd asked for diamond-encrusted cereal. Her plea caught Hamish's attention back from the snow to stand beside his sister.

'They won't be the same, Pops.' The scowl on his face aged him beyond his young years and the scolding soon made Poppy's head drop too.

'I can make pancakes. It's no problem.' Fraser was quick to put any fears to rest and Poppy beckoned him down so she could whisper in his ear. He nodded, took her hand and led her to the kitchen.

'Dad made them shaped like Christmas trees for us.' Hamish's chin wobbled as he explained the significance to Iona.

She put an arm around him and followed the other two. 'Then I'm guessing you'll have to show Fraser exactly how to make them.'

Breakfast was a raucous and messy affair as they all got involved in trying to re-create the perfect tree pancake. This apparently included decorating with a combination of maple syrup and chocolate chips. It wasn't the healthiest start to the day but the sound of their laughter was glorious to hear after last night's unpleasantness.

The sugar rush soon had them bouncing in anticipation of a day playing in the snow and by the time they were bundled up in appropriate layers, Fraser and Iona included, the snow had formed a thick white blanket as far as the eye could see.

They were heading outside when Poppy spotted the mistletoe Fraser had stuck above the door at the last minute.

'You have to kiss Iona!' She clapped her mittened hands together while a disinterested Hamish—with his cast wrapped in a plastic bag so it didn't get wet—went on to make the first footprints in the snow.

To the squealing delight of their little matchmaker, Fraser planted a kiss on Iona's lips and, satisfied he'd fulfilled his obligation, Poppy ran out to join her brother.

Iona tried to follow her out the door, only to be pulled back under the mistletoe.

'Where do you think you're going?'

'Out-outside,' she stuttered, seeing that glint in Fraser's eye that took her right back to what they'd been doing, rolling about on the attic floor.

'Not until I get a proper kiss.'

With the two mischief-makers busy piling snow into the beginnings of a snowman Iona saw no reason to deny herself. Fraser kissed her long and hard and passionately enough that her knees wobbled when she did finally make it outside.

The four of them worked together, rolling and patting mounds of snow into a head and body shape.

'He needs eyes.' Hamish pulled off his glove and used his finger to dig two eyeholes into the blank face.

'Put that back on before you get frostbite and lose the use of that hand too.' Iona wasn't willing to take any more chances when there'd be no clear roads back to the hospital now.

'Can we use these for his mouth and nose?' Poppy opened her hand to display a selection of small shells and stones.

'Where on earth did you find these?' The nearest beach was miles away and they certainly hadn't had the weather recently for a leisurely stroll around the coast.

'They're her lucky finds. She used to collect them when we went beachcombing with Dad and she carries them everywhere.' It was clear Hamish didn't want Poppy to part with them and Iona wouldn't want to deprive her of her link to such precious memories either.

'We could use those, or you could put them back in your pocket and we'll find something else from around here.' She left the decision to Poppy, who stared at the handful of mementoes before stuffing them back into the pocket of her duffel coat, much to Iona's relief.

'Poppy and I are going on a nature hunt, we'll be back soon,' she called to the boys as they headed off to excavate body parts for their new creation. They weren't paying attention, too engrossed in dressing Mr Frosty, as Hamish had named him. Fraser took off his woollen hat and perched it on Frosty's head.

'He needs a scarf too.' Scotland's latest fashion expert stared pointedly at Fraser's neck covering, which he untangled with a sigh. If Iona and Poppy weren't quick he'd be stripped bare and in danger of hypothermia. Only half of that thought was appealing so she grabbed the first things she found and, along with Poppy's new finds, they trudged back.

'There. Excellent job, everyone.' With his twig arms and pine-cone features, Frosty was finally complete, providing a much-needed bonding session for her and the children.

'High five!' It was Fraser who led the call for self-congratulations with the others. When he got to Iona, it wasn't a high-five she got but a face full of snow.

'I. Am. Going. To. Kill. You!' she spluttered through the icy face mask.

Fraser was bent double, laughing with his co-conspirators. Not to be outdone, Iona scooped up a handful of loose snow and stuffed it down the back of his trousers. The snow-in-the-pants dance was the best form of revenge she could have wished for as she watched Fraser trying to get it out without mooning at his impressionable young audience.

Taking their cue from the adults, Hamish and Poppy took off screaming and throwing snowballs at each other.

'I suppose you think you're funny?' Fraser advanced on her, eyes narrowed and lips pressed tightly together.

'Hilarious.' Iona folded her arms, determined to stand her ground, but the second she clocked him scooping up more ammunition she took off, shrieking.

He reached her in seconds to launch another icy attack, this time down the back of her neck. She screamed with shock and the weight of Fraser bundling her down onto the ground. They landed together, panting and laughing and so carefree she didn't care about the cold soaking through her clothes.

Her heart fluttered with the possibilities that lay ahead with this man who understood her need for space and provided a little order in the midst of her chaos.

The sound of a vehicle crunching through the snow interrupted this new discovery and had them scrambling back onto their feet.

'I'll go and see who it is.' The weight and the heat lifted from her chest as Fraser jogged off to open the gates. Their future was on hold so they could deal with whatever new guests had arrived. With the bad weather closing in, there was no way this was a casual visit but Iona had the uncharitable thought she wanted them gone already so they could continue with their Christmas fantasy.

'Hamish! Poppy!' she called to get them back inside the house to get warmed up again while Fraser established what was going on out here.

They were wrapped up in front of the fire in the lounge when he returned with the visitors.

'Mum!' The children flung themselves at Katherine as she walked in, accompanied by an older man and woman.

'Easy.' Fraser stepped in before they knocked her off her feet.

'They didn't tell us you were getting out this morning or we would've had the children ready for you.' Iona was as gobsmacked as the children to see her since they hadn't said anything other than she was improving on her last check. Whilst she was happy for their sakes that they were reunited, she did feel as though she'd been caught out rolling around in the snow with Fraser when they'd arrived.

'My blood pressure's down and Mum and Dad managed to get a flight in this morning. They agreed to let me out as long as I rest, but I wanted to surprise these two.' The colour was back in the young mum's cheeks at having her children back again and Iona wouldn't have denied her a second with them.

'I think you did that all right but you should be taking it easy. Have a seat. Can we get you something to eat or drink?' At least Fraser remembered his manners, playing the host and introducing himself to her parents. Iona was glad the children were going to have their Christmas after all but she had a horrible premonition hers had come to an end.

'I really just want to get home. I'm sure you understand, Iona.'

She did but it didn't make it any easier for her to say goodbye. 'Of course. I'll go and get their things.'

It was silly to get upset when this was the best present the family could have received but it didn't stop the tears falling as she folded their clothes and packed their bags to leave. It marked the end of their pretend family and she didn't know what that meant for her and Fraser.

Iona composed herself when the time came to see them off. It wouldn't have been fair to spoil their moment when they were so happy to be going home together.

'Thank you for everything.' Katherine insisted on hugging her and Fraser as tightly as her huge pregnant belly would allow and Hamish and Poppy followed suit. Iona managed to keep her quivering smile in place until they finally drove away.

'You'll see them again.' Fraser slipped an arm around her waist and held her close.

'I know. It's just…' If she was honest she didn't know why their departure was hitting her so hard other than the absurd notion that he mightn't want her now they weren't part of the package. As if having a ready-made family to fill his house was the only reason he'd fallen for her.

'You got used to having them around? Me too.' Given the noise and disruption two small children managed to make, his admission would've been surprising once upon a time but not any more. Not since she'd seen the tolerant, nurturing side of him that she'd fallen for.

He closed the door on the outside world so there was only the two of them left to fill the home.

'This is our time now and as the lady of the house I wonder if you might care to join me in the master bedroom?'

Her heart wasn't the only part of her flourishing back to life with the promise he was making her. Time alone with him wasn't a luxury she had yet explored to its fullest potential.

'I'm not really looking my best after rolling around in the snow. Perhaps the Laird would prefer to wait for me to freshen up before he ravishes me?' A girl wanted to look her best for such auspicious occasions. Even those where her clothes wouldn't be required for too long.

'The Laird would not. He does, however, think it would be more fun to freshen up together.' He wiggled his eyebrows in a comically suggestive manner, totally unsuitable for a laird or a doctor, which made her laugh and practically run into the master bedroom along with him.

* * *

The Laird's Chamber was as grand and masculine as Iona had imagined, with swathes of tartan and the family crest everywhere to tell the tale of Fraser's heritage. Yet if it had been cast entirely of gold and diamonds she would still have been more impressed with the sight of Fraser undressing in the room.

Without saying a word, he stripped naked, the sound of a bath running the only prompt Iona needed to mirror his moves. There could've been some awkwardness standing here staring at each other's naked bodies but Fraser watched her with so much admiration and desire that any inhibitions were quashed before they had time to manifest themselves. With such a fine body himself, Fraser had nothing to be ashamed of and clearly wasn't, striding confidently to the bathroom.

Iona felt more of a queen than a lady stepping into the cloud of bubbles in the tub, the warm water inviting her to sink deeper. Fraser's long legs enveloped hers and she relaxed back against his chest, letting the water and her lover wash over her.

She couldn't remember the last time anyone outside a salon had washed her hair but he did so, unbidden. He lathered the shampoo in her hair, his fingers massaging her scalp with a tenderness that made her want to weep. By all accounts, no one had ever taken care of him, yet here he was expressing his love for her by touch alone.

She closed her eyes as he rinsed out the suds and though she was content to remain where she was, she was obliged to give him the chance to experience this bliss too. 'Do you want me to wash your hair for you?'

'In a minute. I'm enjoying taking care of you without you trying to bite my head off for it.'

Now she knew there was no call to rebel against him through fear he was trying to get the upper hand over her,

Iona had to admit it was nice having someone look after her. She'd been on her own for so long, untrusting and suspicious, she'd forgotten simple pleasures like this.

Fraser took a flannel and began to wash her body with long, sensual strokes across her neck, over her breasts, slipping further down between her legs. She closed her eyes and gave herself over to his ministrations. After giving so much of herself these past few days, she figured she was entitled to some pampering.

Under the water he continued to move the cloth along her thighs, teasing across the part of her so desperately aching for his touch. She let out a whimper as he abandoned the flannel and carried on, using only his fingers to stroke her.

He kissed his way across her shoulder to that sensitive spot at her neck that automatically increased her arousal tenfold. It was then he pushed inside her, drawing a gasp and a groan as he soothed her ache.

She writhed against him as he stretched and filled her with his fingers, the swell of his erection pressed into the small of her back turning her on beyond measure. He wanted her but he wasn't going to have her until he'd driven her to climax first. A selfless lover was the best aphrodisiac known to womankind.

With one hand pushing her towards the brink of oblivion, the other was at her breast, pinching her nipple to provide that oh-so-pleasurable pain. Her orgasm slammed into her, the blinding flash behind her eyelids and shudder of gratification taking her breath away with the sheer force of it.

She was so lost in that spiralling bliss she didn't realise those erotic cries echoing around the walls were coming from her.

'Are you okay?' Fraser whispered in her ear, his hot

breath sending another aftershock of rapture rippling through her body.

'Uh-huh.' Apart from having lost the power of speech, her mouth dry and her brain having exploded with the sensations he'd drawn from her.

'In that case, let's get you dried off.' Water sluiced over her and the floor as he stood up and that weightlessness in her body disappeared at once.

'What about your hair?' Fraser wasn't going to cheat her out of doing something for him in return. She wanted him to experience the same moment of pure happiness he'd just given her.

'It's not my hair that's needs tending right now.' He grinned and held up a towel, waiting for her to get out of the bath.

There was no place for her gaze to linger other than at his manhood standing tall and demanding her attention.

Fraser swamped her in the fleecy warmth of the bath sheet, carried her into the bedroom and laid her down on the covers as though she was the most precious thing in the world. At that moment that's exactly how he made her feel.

He unwrapped her painfully slowly, taking his time to appreciate every inch of her he uncovered. There was no mistaking his desire for her, it was there for her to see in all its physical glory, but so was the love in his eyes for her, and that was her undoing. Fraser wasn't the same as the others, he wouldn't hurt her or try to change her, and he loved her for who she was, regardless of how difficult it was for him at times. In the few days they'd lived together they'd learned the art of compromise. Learned to love and live in harmony.

It was an unconventional match but it kept things so exciting and passionate between them that Iona never wanted to leave his bed.

Anticipation was throbbing through her body with that

one look promising all the things he was going to do to, and with, her.

She pressed herself tightly into him, teasing them both as her nipples rubbed against his chest and Fraser groaned, his erection grazing where she craved him most. He swallowed her breathy pleas with a tongue-tangling display of desire that did nothing to quench the fiery lust coursing through her veins.

'I need you, Fraser.' She begged him to fill that part of her that was incomplete without him now.

'I need you too.'

They belonged together and now they'd found each other it was unthinkable that they should ever be parted again.

Last night had been the culmination of their pent-up yearning for one another, a frantic endeavour to release that pressure and find ultimate satisfaction as quickly as possible. Being together here, Iona knew, was an expression of the depth of their feelings for one another, tender and loving as they took their time climbing towards that peak of absolute contentment together. It carried them both in quick succession over the finish line, leaving her breathless and euphoric.

She watched the rise and fall of his chest as he lay down beside her and the smile spreading across his face adding his own glowing review of their endeavours.

'Has it—is it—always this way for you?' It was the sort of question one might attribute to a naïve virgin but she'd never experienced this level of impact on her heart and her body.

She'd had lovers and the occasional relationship but none of her previous partners had reached her or taken her to such heights the way Fraser had. It made her question if she'd truly been in love before or if he was simply an exceptional lover. Perhaps he had this effect on every woman who'd ever shared his bed but she wanted what they had to be special for him too.

Fraser rolled over onto his side, propping his head on his hand, and reached out to brush a tendril of her still-wet hair from her face. She turned her cheek into his palm and closed her eyes, afraid to know the answer in case it ruined this for ever.

'Never.' His soft voice reached in behind her closed lids and travelled all the way to her soul. He was hers and hers alone and if every time was like this she never wanted to wake up alone again.

CHAPTER ELEVEN

IT WAS DARK when they finally decided to leave bed in search of sustenance. Iona walked over to the window to close the curtains and found the world outside glowing with a fresh fall of snow.

'Winter has well and truly arrived.' The night was so peaceful and still, they could've been perched atop their own private glacier, miles from civilisation, and content to be so.

'In that case, we should stock up on food supplies to see us through our hibernation.' Fraser jumped out of bed and began to pull on his clothes.

'What are you doing?' She was dismayed that he was hiding his beautiful body back under layers of fabric when it was so unnecessary.

'Er…getting dressed so we can go down and get something to eat.' The absurdity of what he was doing was completely lost on him so Iona took it upon herself to make the point. She walked over to his side of the bed, making no attempt to hide her own nakedness, and began to unbutton his trousers.

'This is your house, Fraser. We're alone and there's no one around for miles. We don't need clothes.' He put up no objections to her pulling his trousers off—indeed, he appeared very happy to let her do so. There was hope yet he'd learn to abandon some of his stuffy ways with her to lead him astray.

* * *

Fraser approved of Iona's naturist tendencies and with her every effort she was making this into a place he was comfortable to be in. It was early days to bring up the idea of her moving in when she'd barely unpacked in her own flat but she was the sole reason he'd decided he was going to stay in this house.

Iona would certainly blow away the cobwebs here and shake things up as she had done for him. A lot of his old habits and compulsions for order no longer seemed important and no longer dictated his daily schedule. They were no competition when pitted against spending time with Iona instead. With her by his side it was as if his brain had been reset, no longer conditioned to worry about the consequences of every tiny action. It could take a while for him to be a live-in-the-moment kind of guy but with Iona's infectious zest for life he would get there.

They stole downstairs, laughing in the faces of his staid ancestors and making him feel like the naughty child he'd never been here. He'd never done anything intentionally to upset his parents or Caroline. His inability to change had inevitably pushed her away but he'd changed for Iona after only a short time together. Deep down he must have known Caroline wasn't the one for him.

'Houston, we have a problem.' Iona flicked the light switch on and off in the kitchen but they remained in darkness. It was the same in the living room, their beautiful Christmas tree shrouded in shadow instead of twinkling fairy lights. The only light was coming from the fireplace, which would also be their only heat supply too until the power came back on.

'The storm must have brought the lines down. Not to worry, we have plenty of candles.' All those elaborate candelabra around the house would come in useful after all.

'I take it the oven's out of use too?' The desperate call

for food from Iona's rumbling belly was the only downside to the situation but Fraser was used to stocking up for those late nights when he came home and couldn't face cooking.

'Ah, but we do have a selection of cheeses and cold meats. Speaking of which, as much as I appreciate the view, without central heating there's a danger of us contracting pneumonia.' Fraser stacked plate upon plate and loaded a tray up with goodies to take into the lounge and spread out their makeshift picnic in front of the fireplace. Iona snagged the throw from the back of the couch and draped it around their shoulders as she sat down beside him.

It was moments such as this, wrapped up with his lover, feeding each other sustenance after a day spent in bed, that were worth more than money could ever buy.

'Is it wrong of me to want the snowstorm to last for ever so we can stay holed up here?' Iona took a sip from the bottle of water he'd taken from the fridge and a trickle of condensation splashed onto her chest and over her now erect nipple.

'I'd say that sounds perfect.' He leaned down and lapped the droplet with his tongue, thirst quickly overtaking his hunger.

Since having Iona here, he'd decided to make this his permanent residence but it only felt like a home with her in it. If she'd taught him anything over these past days it was to stop over-analysing everything and do what made him happy. He knew they'd only been together a short time, most of that accompanied by two minors, but it was sufficient to know this was right. It wasn't fair to keep ignoring his feelings any more when it had already cost him so much wasted time. 'Why don't you move in?'

Iona's brow knitted together in an expression that showed anything but enthusiasm for the idea. 'I know it's a big house but in case you haven't noticed, I've been living here for a few days now.'

'Well, I didn't think it was the Christmas elves who'd taken over... Seriously, though, think about it, but not for too long. I don't want to waste any more time. I want to be with you, Iona, share this house, and my life, with you.' He'd been here before with Caroline but this was different. He was being truer to himself than he'd ever been, putting everything he was on the line for Iona when he'd never done it for Caroline.

Sweat broke out over his skin the longer he waited for an answer when he'd thought the idea was a no-brainer. They were good for each other, anyone could see that, and their time together in the bedroom, and on the attic floor, had been every bit as exciting as the emotional connection they'd made.

'Fraser...that's—that's...' She was clearly as overwhelmed as he was, struggling to find words.

He knew he was risking a lot on what was primarily a gut instinct they would make this work. The opposite strategy from how he usually lived his life. Iona wasn't the kind of person to be blinded by the expensive trappings that came with him and he trusted her enough to base her decision on the strength of her feelings for him alone.

She stood up, wrapping the blanket around her to cover her nakedness, and Fraser rose with her for the warm hug he anticipated along with her acceptance.

'That's a ridiculous idea.'

He'd stepped towards her before the words slammed into his chest, causing serious internal damage. Optimism and a pitiful hold on the last vestige of hope he could rescue the situation and his heart prevailed. 'I know it's a bit out there but it seems like a natural progression to me when we already know we make a great team. You can ditch that dingy flat, move in here—'

'Quit my job, pop out a couple of kids…' Her tone definitely wasn't in keeping with his earnest endeavour to show her how he felt about her.

'I would never ask you to leave work but I won't lie, I'd like to be a father someday.' He hadn't been thinking quite that far ahead but since she'd brought the subject up he wanted to be honest about his dreams for a family. It had been the deal breaker for Caroline but the way Iona looked after all the children who came into her care hadn't gone unnoticed. He could see a future with her or else he would never have asked her and risked another rejection.

'Fraser, I've only just moved into my own place. You know what it means to me to have my independence. If you're expecting me to sacrifice everything I am for your benefit then you don't know me at all.' Despite everything they'd shared, it appeared Iona was still unwilling to compromise anything for him. Clearly he'd completely misjudged the situation and the baggage she had yet to unpack from her previous relationship if she didn't warrant him worthy of a permanent place in her life. A common theme unfortunately being played out again by someone he loved.

'I was merely asking if you wanted to move in. I've got my answer. That's fine. It was just a thought. Forget I said anything.' Fraser didn't want to cause a row or make her think he was anything akin to her ex when all he'd done was act on impulse. An area in which he apparently still had some work to do.

'No, Fraser. I can't forget it. This is exactly what I was afraid would happen. One small opening into my life and you try to bulldoze through everything. I think we've probably got caught up in this fantasy life we've built around the kids. Let's be honest, before them we didn't really have a lot in common or much to say to one another that wasn't an insult.

'Now they've gone I think we're clutching at straws in

an attempt to keep the fairy-tale going by jumping into bed. But it's not real. I think we've both been too damaged to ever make this work. You need someone here to give you that security you've missed and I can't give up my freedom when it's all I have. I'm going to pack my stuff and go and we'll keep this time together as a fond memory.'

She turned away from him and he knew this was more than a lovers' tiff, she was serious about leaving him and was trying to reduce what they had to a casual fling.

Fraser willed his feet to move, to run after her and beg her to stay but his body was uncooperative, shut down in a complete state of shock. The whole scene was a re-enactment of last year with Caroline, except this was so much more traumatic. Although he hadn't been with Iona long, he knew beyond doubt he was in love with her in a way he'd never loved anyone before. The rejection was not only of him in his truest form but the idea of a future together. Now he'd seen a glimpse of the family and home they could've had together here, he'd never want it with anyone other than Iona.

Nausea undulated through his body as his whole world collapsed around him once more. He reminded himself he was a grown man now, not that little boy who'd been parted from everything he loved without a say. Although Iona's decision to walk out felt very much like being abandoned all over again.

Iona was breathing heavily, her chest tightening with every step she took upstairs to escape the life Fraser was trying to create around her.

Yes, she fancied him like crazy and was maybe even falling in love with him, but the second her defences were down he'd swooped in and tried to exploit that weakness. Living together? Babies? That was a one-way ticket back to that prison she'd broken out of once already.

Iona needed to get back to her own place, her own space, where she could think clearly without abject terror clouding her judgement. Cooped up here, fostering that idea of family with Fraser and the children had messed with both of their heads. Once she was out of the picture again he'd realise that himself. Hopefully by the time they were back at work after the Christmas break they'd remember who they were.

Iona dressed quickly, gathering her belongings as she whipped around the bedroom. If she didn't leave now there was every chance she'd end up back in bed with him at some point and completely forget why her 'dingy flat', complete with borrowed furniture, should be more appealing than Fraser's bed.

It was far too tempting to ignore the distant sound of her phone ringing but she was never really off duty and a call this late could be an emergency.

'Hello.' Her response to whoever was on the line may as well have been an expletive she said it with such aggression but she wasn't in the best of moods, having just ended a relationship with a man she'd come to care for deeply.

'Iona, this is June Lowe, the community midwife on call. I'm sorry to phone out of hours but I understand you're staying with Dr McColl at present and we have an emergency out there. Claire McKenzie is desperately in need of assistance but the main roads there are blocked with fallen trees and downed power lines. We're trying to get an air ambulance out but with the storm... Anyway, we were wondering if you could get through from your end to check on her?'

Iona didn't want to spend long analysing what scenario the rumour mill had dreamed up for Fraser and her being shacked up here together when they would be correct in all of their assumptions. They were consenting adults and it shouldn't matter to anyone else what they did in their private lives as long as it didn't impact on their professional duties. Which it would have done had she not just called a halt to everything.

'Give me the details.' She grabbed a pen and paper from the bedside table and jotted down everything June told her.

Fraser appeared at the door but she didn't have time to feel bad about the forlorn look she'd put on his face.

She put her hand over the phone to let him know what was going on. 'There's a patient in trouble. Claire McKenzie's in advanced labour and her last child was stillborn. I have to get to her. She's not far from here anyway.'

Once she hung up, she forced on her boots and prepared to brave the outdoors.

'Geographically, yes, but we're under several feet of snow in the middle of nowhere. It's not easy terrain to negotiate.'

'I do this for a living, don't forget.' She grabbed her coat and bag, fully aware of the dangers she faced as she walked to her car but nothing was going to stop her from getting to her patient.

'You can't go in that. You'll never make it down the lane.' Fraser insisted on following her outside, criticising her every move.

The compact car was ideal for village life, although probably not conducive to extreme weather conditions, but she didn't have a choice right now.

'Please don't tell me what to do when it comes to my job.' It was easier to leave him when he was trying to undermine her and she started the car regardless of his concerns.

She could see him give chase in her rear-view mirror as the gates opened and she drove away with tears in her eyes and lead in her stomach.

Even at a snail's pace the car tyres slipped and skidded down the lane, gaining no traction at all on the ice, and she was helpless as the vehicle veered off the road and into a ditch.

Before she'd had time to assess any damage to the car, or her pride, she heard the sound of Fraser's four-by-four making its way down the road towards her. Given the circumstances, Iona was going to have to set aside her personal differences with him in order to do her duty to her patient. She'd make sure he didn't take that as a sign she was willing to give him another chance when that was a weakness that had seen her burned too many times.

Once they'd transferred her equipment from the boot of her car into Fraser's I-told-you-so-mobile, Iona got in the passenger side and slammed the door. 'Don't say a word.'

She was in a bad enough mood without another lecture. In the space of fifteen minutes she'd been reminded none of this fairy-tale romance was real, that this relationship couldn't survive reality.

CHAPTER TWELVE

THEY HAD SOME hairy moments during the journey to the patient's house, despite Fraser's careful and methodical driving. There were times when even he couldn't control what happened as the car hit a patch of black ice but the lack of other vehicles in the area at least prevented any serious accident.

If pushed, Iona would have admitted his jeep was better equipped for the road conditions than her runabout, but she didn't think the choice of driver made a difference regardless of Fraser's opinion on the subject. He could have easily handed his keys over to her and gone home but that apparently wasn't something he had been ready to do.

'That's the McKenzie place up there.'

They were forced to stop at the bottom of a particularly hilly stretch of road, their journey brought to an end by the huge tree and assorted debris strewn across their route. The McKenzies' car had been abandoned halfway between the obstacles and their house.

'Could you help me carry my equipment up to the house, please?' Iona could have been churlish and insist she manage on her own, leaving Fraser freezing down here, but that wouldn't achieve anything. By giving him a task, it was also asserting her position in this situation. She was in charge.

'No problem.' He fell into line and Iona loaded him up with any kit she might need. Only time would tell how long this compliance would last once they were confronted with whatever was going on behind that front door.

Mr McKenzie met them at the door, wearing the pan-icked face of a father-to-be. 'Thank goodness you're here. The baby's on its way. We can't get out and after last time…' He didn't have to say any more as he ran a shak-ing hand through his hair. Claire had recounted to her the trauma the family had gone through in her last pregnancy, which had ended in the stillbirth of their precious baby. Despite reassurances there was no medical reason the same would happen again, the couple had been understandably anxious for the duration of this pregnancy and this setback wasn't going to allay any of those fears. That was her job.

'Where's Claire? I'll have to examine her and see what stage we're at.' Nothing else could be helped now and the importance of mother and baby's welfare had to come be-fore anything. If they were trapped up here for the entirety of her labour, Iona had to be prepared for any eventuality.

'She's up in the bedroom. Said she was in too much pain to try and get out again.' The understandably anxious birthing partner led them up to what was about to become the delivery suite, but he was so tense Iona wasn't con-vinced he'd do anything to put his wife at ease.

Regardless of the urgency in the situation, Iona took the time to knock on the door and introduce herself. 'It's Iona. The midwife.'

It was important patients maintain some dignity and privacy where they could so they weren't made to feel little more than a baby-making machine in the process.

'Come in. I'm so glad you're here.' Claire's fears were evident as she welcomed her into the room. Iona didn't know any more than the rest how this was going to play out but she had to act as confidently as she could manage to keep Claire calm. Stress could cause more complications if her blood pressure spiked now and there was only so much Iona could do without the conveniences of a hospital labour ward.

'You've got a midwife and a GP on hand so there's no cause for alarm. Now, how far apart are the contractions?' She left the two men hovering in the doorway to come and examine her patient.

'It feels as though they're constant.' Claire groaned as her belly tightened with another.

'Every two minutes. I was timing them before you came,' Craig chimed in.

'In that case, baby shouldn't be too long.' Iona wasn't worried about delivering the baby at home, she'd done it plenty of times, but she usually had more time to prepare. Especially if there'd been complications in previous pregnancies.

'What if the same thing happens again? Instead of bringing our baby home last time, all we had was a memory box. If something goes wrong here…'

Iona understood Craig's concerns and she'd had the same thought herself but there was nothing they could do but deliver the baby into the world. This constant reminder of their loss was going to prevent Claire taking any good memories from this labour and she had to get him out. He could be a part of the birth experience when the time came but for now it was better for all concerned if he took a back seat.

'We'll have it covered. Fraser, why don't you go and stick the kettle on for all of us? There's a gas cooker downstairs if you don't mind making it the old-fashioned way. Craig can fill you in and I'll get Claire comfortable here.' The message to Fraser was twofold, get Craig out of here and if I need your help I'll ask for it.

As one might have predicted, he wasn't prepared to relinquish the medical lead as easily as that.

'Craig, if you could do the honours, I'd like to have a word with Iona first.' His lips were drawn into a tight line, such a contrast to the soft mouth that had covered her body with tender kisses only hours earlier.

Iona trusted he wasn't so blinded by ego he couldn't see the serene atmosphere she was trying to create here, but she did step out onto the landing to have the conversation in private.

'What's up? I'm kind of busy here.' She kept one hand on the doorknob, making it clear she wasn't going to be detained long.

'I know you're ticked off at me but please let me help.' He could have called her out on the fact she'd relegated him to tea boy, put on some display of anger towards her based on the way she'd treated him since he'd asked her to move in with him. Instead, she could see he simply wanted them both to work together for the best outcome.

'I know what I'm doing but if I need you I promise I'll call.' Thinking of Claire lying behind the door, already afraid of what was going to happen, she knew she couldn't let her personal problems jeopardise the labour should anything go wrong out here.

'Thank you.'

She couldn't resist one last needle before she went back into the bedroom and closed the door. 'Mine's milk with one sugar, thanks.'

At least now she couldn't see or hear him she could get on with her job and bring this baby safely into the world.

'Okay, Claire, I'm just going to do a wee check and see how dilated you are.'

Dismissed from the scene, Fraser was forced to join the anxious Craig downstairs, cursing Iona for her pigheadedness. All he wanted to do was protect her, not that he could tell her that when she'd made it clear she thought he was trying to take over her life.

'Tea or coffee?' Craig greeted him at the bottom of the stairs, clutching a jar of coffee and a teabag.

'Neither. Have you got a snow shovel or heavy chains or something?' Fraser wanted to be more pro-active than simply sitting here, sipping tea.

Rather than rushing off to source essential tools to dig them out of here, Craig was still staring at him blankly, choice of beverages in hand.

It was tempting to try and shake some urgency into him but there was no need to see another display of his headless-chicken routine. He needed clear direction and something constructive to keep him occupied.

'Teatime can wait. We could be doing something useful, such as trying to move that tree. Your wife and child are going to need a clear path out of here at some point.'

That evocative reminder of why they were all here galvanised Craig into action. He turned back into the kitchen and tossed the tea things on the worktop. Iona probably wouldn't have liked the way he made it anyway.

'I'll take a look in the shed and see what I've got.'

'Great. At least then we'll feel as though we're doing something to help.' Iona mightn't want him here in a personal capacity but he could still be useful. With any luck they would all come out of this unscathed then he could set his mind to trying to win her back.

The sounds of scraping and revving car engines outside weren't going to distract Iona. Whatever Fraser was up to, at least it was keeping him out of her business. She had enough to deal with here, without dealing with Fraser's ego too.

It had become clear Claire's contractions had been going

on for some time with little progress. On examination she'd detected a problem that could explain the delay.

'Claire, I think the baby is in what we call the asynclitic position, where baby should come into the pelvis and rotate into position but in this case the head hasn't engaged properly. That's putting pressure on your pubic bone too.' There were certain positions with the foetal head that couldn't be delivered vaginally, which would be grave cause for concern here without proper intervention They were going to have to go back to basics to try and get the baby moving to where it needed to be.

'What do we do?' Claire's sobs were a mixture of fear and exhaustion, her hair stuck to her face with sweat, labour taking its toll. There were still a few tricks Iona could try to get junior to move before there was any reason to start stressing.

'I can tell you what we're not going to do, we're not going to panic. I'm going to go and see what's keeping your husband with the tea and get him to give us a hand to direct baby to the way out.' The attempt at humour took some of the focus off potential danger. Whatever happened, Claire was going to need the support of her husband to get through it, and despite Iona's resistance to engage Fraser in proceedings she would require his assistance if the baby was in distress.

She didn't waste any time locating the men, following the racket outside.

'Both of you come upstairs, now.' She had to yell to get their attention they were so engrossed in clearing the snow from the road.

'Is something wrong?' Craig came running first, with Fraser close behind, his cheeks so pink with cold it made her yearn for that time they'd spent wrapped up in front of the fire. It was too bad she'd learned the hard way there was no point in looking back.

'Baby needs some encouragement to move into place so Claire's going to need some assistance to get into a better position. She's a bit emotional right now so it would be good if you could just reassure her and support her through the contractions in the meantime.'

Fraser hung back to discuss the matter out of Craig's earshot. 'We've cleared a path down to my car. We could try to get her down.'

Iona shook her head. 'We're way past that stage. You're going to have to take my word for it, she's not going anywhere. Unfortunately, neither is the baby. Now, if you really want to help you can come up and run her a nice warm bath.'

She wasn't going to hang around to argue the point. The baby was dictating what happened here, not her and certainly not Fraser.

'We're going to move you so you're on all fours, Claire. It might help tilt the baby's head forward. Craig, can you give me a hand here to move the pillows and get her more comfortable?'

Between them they manoeuvred Claire onto her hands and knees, with the pillows to cushion the front of her body. She was too exhausted to put all the weight on her arms, panting through each contraction with Craig rubbing her back and making encouraging murmurs. It must be nice to have a supportive partner willing you on through such a momentous event but Iona doubted she'd ever experience it through any stage of her life.

'How's she doing?' Fraser wandered in, drying his hands on a towel, having actually followed instructions and drawn a bath for Claire.

'Working hard. Claire, could we get you into the bath for a while? It's not the traditional birthing pool but it might relax you and encourage our long-awaited arrival to drop down.'

Once the next contraction passed they had a small window to make the move before the next one hit. They encouraged her to lean over the edge of the bath in much the same position as she'd been on the bed. It was a tight squeeze with the four of them in the bathroom but they were all working towards the same outcome.

'You're doing great, Claire.' Iona reached down with the Doppler device so she could listen to the baby's heartbeat, which was still fast and strong.

Craig was holding her hand and helping her to pant through the contractions and Fraser was scooping warm water over her back so she didn't get cold.

As the contractions became more powerful it became increasingly clear the baby was finally ready to make an appearance. They had to wait for that brief respite again before transporting her back and in the end the birth was quick, Iona catching him before he slid onto the bed.

'Daddy, would you like to cut the cord?'

'We did it, Claire. We have a son.' Happy tears were streaming down the proud father's face as he did the honours.

Iona placed the baby on the mother's chest so they had that precious first skin-to-skin contact, welling up herself now that the danger had passed and he was finally here. It was always a privilege to be part of people's lives and follow their journey, more so to see it through to a happy end.

'Congratulations. All of you.' Fraser's praise was welcome but it was also tinged with a little sadness for Iona because when this was over she was faced with the prospect of going home. Alone.

Once she was sure the baby's Apgar score determined it was in good health they could leave the couple to enjoy the new member of their family until the next check-up.

A low score now would suggest baby needed extra medical care but indications so far were good.

'Iona?' Fraser no longer sounded full of the joys of a new baby but concerned as he drew her attention to the scarlet stain spreading rapidly across the bed covers, enough to suggest a post-partum haemorrhage.

She nodded an acknowledgement, trying not to scare the McKenzies, but the amount of blood being lost constituted an emergency. Even when births seemed to go to plan they were notoriously unpredictable. These days a woman was very unlikely to bleed to death giving birth, but this hadn't been a planned home delivery and currently they had no way to get her to hospital where they would be best equipped to deal with all eventualities.

'Okay, Claire, you're losing quite a lot of blood and we need to find the source so we can deal with it as quickly as possible. Craig, could you go and phone for an ambulance again and see what's happening out there?' She remained calm and in control of the situation for the benefit of the new parents, who were currently wide-eyed with fear, even though her own pulse was hammering away with the implications of the situation.

'Do you need me to take the baby?' Craig dithered by the bedside, ignoring her request. Thankfully Fraser had his mobile in his pocket so he went ahead and phoned in the emergency. In hindsight it was probably best to have him chasing up some medical support when he understood the severity of the situation.

'It would actually help contract the uterus if we could get the baby to breast feed. Do you think you could try that, Claire?'

She nodded, and with her husband's assistance they tried to get the baby to latch on, leaving Iona the important job of finding out why this had happened using the *T*s—tissue, tone, trauma and thrombin. She hadn't needed stitches so that ruled out trauma, and thrombin, an issue with blood clotting, was rare and would've been known prior to birth. Although the placenta had been delivered there was a chance a bit had been left behind or that the uterus didn't have enough tone to contract and stop the bleeding.

They might not be in a conventional hospital setting but she would follow the same steps regardless. She encouraged Claire to pass urine so she didn't have a full bladder and massaged the top of her uterus to stimulate it to contract, but blood was still gushing at an alarming rate.

'They're on their way. What can I do?' Thank goodness Fraser was here, offering another pair of hands where she desperately needed them.

'I'm going to administer an oxytocic drug but if that doesn't stop the bleeding we should put up an IV. Everything we need is in my bag.' Ordinarily the drugs were enough but if they had to transfer her to the hospital they needed a vein open and ready for easy access if necessary. Any issues with clotting would need to be treated and blood products administered.

With Fraser available to set up the IV, Iona was able to continue to massage the uterus in the hope it might help expel any retained tissue preventing good uterine clampdown.

'You're doing great.' Fraser was doing a good job of re-assuring Claire everything was going to be all right, then Iona felt the warmth of his hand on her back and she realised he was talking to her.

That unexpected support when she was so accustomed of weathering the storm alone almost made her cry at his kindness after the way she'd treated him today. She knew in that moment that no matter what happened between them romantically, he'd always be there, supporting her. It put her earlier rant into perspective and her hysteria that he was somehow trying to railroad her into another painful relationship. Fraser would never hurt her. She'd simply been projecting her own fears onto him because she was so afraid of making another mistake.

She couldn't bring herself to respond to him, afraid she'd burst into tears and never regain her composure at a time it was needed more than ever. Instead, she continued bi-manual compression, continually pushing on the uterus externally and internally until they heard the sound of the ambulance siren in the distance and she nearly collapsed with relief.

'I couldn't stop the bleeding, Fraser.' Iona was beside him, watching the ambulance make its way cautiously back down the path he and Craig had shovelled, with the McKenzies loaded up inside.

'You did everything possible. You were amazing. I'm sure she's going to be fine, thanks to your actions.' If Claire required a blood transfusion or surgery to remove any remaining placenta, it was down to the hospital staff now to continue her treatment. Iona had done her best given the circumstances and he was proud of how she'd handled everything in such a potentially life-threatening situation.

It was easy to take midwives for granted when he wasn't actively involved with their practices every day, but having now seen first-hand how fraught a home birth could be, Fraser respected her even more. Especially since she didn't seem to have the confidence in her actions that she'd portrayed to the worried couple. He was sure her calm exterior had prevented them all from losing it and making matters worse, even if her own stress levels had been through the roof.

'I'm glad you were there with me. I couldn't have done it without your help.' After their earlier parting, Iona's words meant more to him than ever. He hoped in some small way he'd shown her he'd never do anything to interfere in her life and only wished to be part of it in some way.

'I'm pretty sure you could. You've managed all this time without me. Now, let's get back to my place out of this cold.' He understood where she was coming from. They were both perfectly capable of doing their jobs on their own but there was something reassuring about having that extra body nearby in case they were needed. It took the pressure off when you were able to share the experience with someone who understood the situation on the front line of medicine.

Neither of them had to go through life alone, if only they'd open up and accept they deserved the kind of love and support they could offer each other. It was something they really should discuss back at his place if Iona was willing to hear him out.

'Well, my car is still in a ditch there so I suppose I'll have to go with you.' That hesitation remained but she did lift her bag, indicating she would follow him.

He saw her legs begin to buckle as the enormity of the day seemed to hit her all at once. She wasn't as immune to the stress of the ordeal as she pretended. Not that anyone else would have known as she'd waited until her patient was safe before she'd given in to her own feelings. On this occasion at least she didn't have to go through it alone. He swooped down and scooped her up into his arms, just like that first time they'd found themselves thrown together.

'What are you doing?' Iona put up a half-hearted protest but he could tell she no longer had the strength to fight and that in itself was cause for concern.

'I don't care if you hate me for it but someone has to look after you. You're exhausted and in need of a strong cup of tea.' Everything else could wait until he was certain she had recovered from the trauma of the birth herself.

The drive back was as quiet as the outward journey had

been but the atmosphere seemed more of a comfortable silence than the frosty drive out to the McKenzies' place.

'I'll get your car fixed up for you later,' he promised as they passed her abandoned vehicle.

'I can do it myself. I was just in a hurry to get to Claire earlier.' Even in her current state she was asserting that independence at any cost.

Fraser sighed. He couldn't understand why she didn't see he only ever wanted to help but he wasn't going to get into another argument with her now.

They pulled up outside the house and he went around to Iona's side of the car to help her out.

'I can walk, thanks.'

'Sure.' Glad she was coming inside at least, Fraser gave her some space and went on ahead.

The scene greeting them in the living room was like something out of a tragedy. The power was back on, the Christmas tree twinkling in the corner of the room and illuminating the remnants of their post-coital picnic on the floor. It was a reminder of the happy times they'd had together and those they could still have together.

Everywhere he went in the house Fraser would be faced with more painful memories. Except now they'd be full of Iona's smile, her kiss and the sense of having her close to him.

The room smelled of Iona's sweet perfume and Christmas and he knew packing away those decorations she'd so lovingly hung for the children would kill him. All the fairy-lights and mistletoe would now become symbols of loss and regret.

Fraser thought of the pain caused by his parents never truly opening up about their feelings to him. If only they'd been able to talk things over, at any stage of his life, it could have saved them all a lot of heartache. He understood now they had been trying to protect him in their own way, but by shutting him out he'd only imagined the worst. They'd missed out on so much, all for the want of better communication. Such a waste of precious time that could have been spent together in his mother's last days. Perhaps he would've even been reconciled with his father at the end of his life too.

He didn't want to make the same mistakes with Iona when she meant so much to him, and he wasn't prepared to give up on love without a fight. This house was a shell without her in it and he could never be happy here alone.

'Please don't go, Iona. Can't we just start again?'

'We're so different...' Instead of the definitive no she'd given him earlier, she seemed to be mulling over the idea of a second chance. Perhaps the visual reminder of their time here had had a similar impact on her too.

'We've known that from the start. That's what makes the sparks fly, remember?' Life would never be boring between them and he wanted to remind her that their personality clashes could be a whole lot of fun at times.

Iona managed a wistful smile. 'Passion might disguise the real problems for a while but they show themselves in the end. I can't be with someone who thinks they can run my life for me. I'm never getting into that kind of toxic relationship again.'

'I would never try to control you. In my clumsy way I was trying to show you how much I cared for you.' Fraser's stomach rolled as he realised his misplaced faith in rules and order had fed directly into Iona's fears about everything she thought he represented from her past, and he didn't know how to fix it. Nothing meant as much to him as Iona and he'd give up anything for one more chance to prove it.

Previous experience had shown Iona that controlling men didn't change their behaviour for anyone. They might pretend for a while to be charming and contrite but that was all part of their manipulation. Their way of maintaining a hold on their victims by showing they were capable of redemption but always under an atmosphere of fear. Her mother had been afraid of her father and Iona would've left her ex sooner if not for the underlying threat of violence. She'd never once been afraid of Fraser. Annoyed, frustrated and downright angry at times with him but never had she seriously considered that by voicing her opinion on anything he would do her harm.

'It took a lot for me to walk away from the last man who tried to control me and it's taken me years to get where I am now. I have no intention of going back there.' Despite how desperately she longed to rewind time back to when they had been wrapped up here together with the world at their feet.

'I'm sorry. Did your ex ever say that to you and mean it? I'm truly sorry.'

Iona had heard the words before but never with the genuine remorse she saw shining in Fraser's eyes.

'I'm afraid to put myself in that position again when my life is very much my own now.'

'And you're not willing to share it with me at least? That's all I'm asking, Iona. I love you. If nothing else I want you to know that and believe it.' The catch in his voice gave away the truth of what he was saying and though hearing it made her heart soar and gave validation to her feelings for him, it couldn't completely heal her scars.

She wasn't used to having someone looking out for her unless they were trying to use it against her for their own means.

'In case you missed it, I'll say it again. I love you, Iona. I want us to be together.'

She was afraid that if she told him how much her heart

was swelling with love for him too she might start ugly crying again and he might change his mind about loving her.

'Asking you to move in here, I suppose, was symbolic. I was offering my heart along with the key to my home. I mean, we can forget the whole living-together thing. I know you just moved into your own place. Just tell me you feel the same about me and it'll give me hope I haven't totally messed this up.'

His rambling was endearing and she knew he'd never try to force her into doing anything when he was doing his best to give her her own space. Today had shown how much he loved her even before he'd said it out loud. Not only had he been there to assist her during Claire's labour in a professional capacity, but he'd been an invaluable source of emotional support to her. Something she hadn't realised she'd been missing until he'd rubbed her back and reassured her she was doing everything right.

His kindness in the face of her hostility towards him said everything about his character that she needed to know. It made her see her reaction towards his offer had been because she'd feared the strength of her own feelings for him, brainwashed by past experiences into thinking it meant she was opening herself up to get hurt again. She was still letting Andy isolate her from people who really loved her.

Iona would never love anyone the way she loved Fraser for everything he'd done for her, and how he loved her. He'd gone against all his own fears to open his house up to her and the children, had decorated for Christmas regardless of his own personal issues and had abandoned his rule book so they had all been comfortable here. He'd sacrificed a lot to try and make her happy.

So she had two options. She could throw herself wholeheartedly into a relationship with him and take the risk along with him that love would win out and make everything worthwhile. Or she could walk away now and protect what was left of her heart, back to the safe life she'd left behind in her one-bedroom flat. If she wanted to live life to the fullest she could no longer hide away from everything it had to offer.

She leaned in to whisper in his ear, 'I love you too.'

As the truth left her lips that veil of suspicion finally lifted. She loved him with every fibre of her being. Fraser McColl was the part of her she hadn't realised was missing until she'd tried to walk away from him.

He gathered her up in his arms and peppered her with kisses. 'You don't know how happy that makes me.'

She had a fair idea with the grip he had on her and the size of the grin on his face. 'Is that offer to move in still on the table?'

He stopped hugging and kissing her long enough to stare. 'Does this mean—?'

'Yes. I want to live with you. I want to spend Christmas here with you and every day after that if you still want me.' There was that slight wobble in confidence that he might have grown tired of her drama.

'Always,' he said, and planted one of those delicious long kisses on her lips.

Fraser McColl was the best Christmas present she could ever have wished for.

EPILOGUE

'OKAY, THE TREE'S UP, the dinner's in the oven and we have cover for the holidays. Is there anything we've forgotten?'

Fraser had his hands on his head, searching his mind for things they might still have to do, but Iona was certain they'd made provision for every possible eventuality.

'Relax. They're going to be here soon and we don't want you stressing them out. This isn't our first rodeo, remember?' Iona handed him some fresh towels to set out in preparation for their new arrivals so he had something to keep him busy other than driving her mad with his constant worrying.

'No, but it is our first *official* Christmas as foster parents. I want everything to be right for them.' Fraser's compassion for the unfortunate children who'd found themselves in the care system through no fault of their own hadn't lessened over the years and she loved him for it.

'It will be.' She kissed him gently on the lips, hoping it would go some way to settling his nervous excitement. He always gave one hundred percent to the children who came to stay with them, no matter how short their time here, but Christmas was particularly special to him as he wanted to give them the special memories he hadn't had as a youngster. After their experiences with Hamish and Poppy they'd both been keen to offer the same safe environment to others and it had given him a reason to keep on the family home other than through obligation alone.

Iona had moved in shortly after their first Christmas together, shipping her barely opened boxes from her beloved apartment, but Fraser had never put her under pressure to do anything she didn't want to. When it came to those big decisions they always had a lengthy conversation so there was no room for misunderstanding and it had worked out pretty well for them so far. They'd taken their time with their relationship, only committing to marriage when they had both been ready, and doing it on the quiet because it was for no one else's benefit but their own.

Since then it had been a whirlwind of activity in the big house, redecorating and turning the place into a home where everyone was welcome. A family remained on the agenda for both of them but for now they were content to parent on a temporary basis for those who needed it.

'Here they come.' Fraser set the towels on the hall table to open the door for the terrified little faces peeking out from the back of the car pulling up in the drive. He wrapped a hand around Iona's waist and pulled her close, their united front to put the eight-year-old twin girls at ease as they ventured towards the strange new house. His heart was so full of love to give to these children for whom it had been so lacking, Iona knew it wouldn't be long before they started their own family. Fraser had proved time and time again he'd make as good a father as he did a husband. For now, though, these children were theirs to look after and nurture until their circumstances improved, and they'd devote all of their time and energy into doing that.

'Have I told you how much I love you?' she whispered to her husband, doting on him more every time she witnessed his devotion to helping others.

'Not in the last five minutes.' He grinned and left one

last, lingering kiss on her lips before their visitors came to meet them.

'Welcome.'

'Merry Christmas.'

They greeted their new family with warm smiles and a desire to make some new, cosy Christmas memories with them to last a lifetime. It was only right they should share their happiness with those less fortunate when they had so much of it to give.

* * * * *

COMING SOON!

We really hope you enjoyed reading this book. If you're looking for more romance, be sure to head to the shops when new books are available on

Thursday 29th November

To see which titles are coming soon, please visit
millsandboon.co.uk

MILLS & BOON

Coming next month

THE BILLIONAIRE'S CHRISTMAS WISH
Tina Beckett

'Theo?'

'Actually, I'm struggling with something.' Maybe it was the revelations about her mom that cast Madison in a different light—the reasons for the slight standoffishness he'd noticed from time to time suddenly making sense. Or maybe it was the stress of dealing with Ivy's illness that had his senses out of whack. But he found himself wanting to do something crazy and impulsive, something he hadn't analyzed from every angle before acting on it.

'With what?'

'The way your thoughts dart from one thing to the other so fast that I can barely keep up.'

'I—I'm sorry.'

'Don't be. I like it. But it also drives me...insane. In ways I should be able to control.' Letting go of her hand, he curled his fingers around the nape of her neck, his thumb sliding just beneath her jaw to where he knew her pulse beat. He let his fingers trail down the side of her throat, along skin that was incredibly soft. 'But right now I don't want to control it. And that's the struggle. So...I need you to tell me to back off.'

She moistened her lips and started to say something, then stopped. Her eyes met his. 'I don't think I can.'

Something inside him leaped to attention and he lowered his voice, aware that they were still completely alone. 'You can't tell me to back off, or you don't want to?' He leaned forward, employing light pressure to bring her nearer until their lips were a mere centimeter away.

'I don't want to tell you…want you to…' Her hand went to his shoulder, fingers pressing through the thin fabric of his button-down shirt. Warmth bloomed and traveled. And then, with a feeling of déjà vu, her mouth touched his.

Senses that had been dormant for years erupted in a huge array of lights that rendered him blind for several seconds.

When he could see again, he was kissing her back and Theo knew at that moment he was in big trouble. He should stop this before it went any further, but his limbs wouldn't co-operate. Neither would his mouth.

So there was nothing else to do but sit back and enjoy the ride. Because any time now Madison was sure to realize what a mistake this was and call a screeching halt to it.

All of it.

And when that happened, Theo had no idea what he was going to do.

Continue reading
THE BILLIONAIRE'S CHRISTMAS WISH
Tina Beckett

Available next month
www.millsandboon.co.uk

LET'S TALK
Romance

For exclusive extracts, competitions
and special offers, find us online:

f facebook.com/millsandboon

🐦 @MillsandBoon

📷 @MillsandBoonUK

Get in touch on 01413 063232

For all the latest titles coming soon, visit
millsandboon.co.uk/nextmonth